Insatiable Love 2:

When Broken Hearts Collide

Insatiable Love 2:

When Broken Hearts Collide

Latoya Chandler

www.urbanbooks.net

Urban Books, LLC
300 Farmingdale Road, NY-Route 109
Farmingdale, NY 11735

Insatiable Love 2: When Broken Hearts Collide

ISBN 13: 978-1-64556-322-8
ISBN 10: 1-64556-322-7

First Mass Market Printing September 2022
First Trade Paperback Printing November 2021
Printed in the United States of America

10 9 8 7 6 5 4 3 2 1

Distributed by Kensington Publishing Corp.
Submit Orders to:
Customer Service
400 Hahn Road
Westminster, MD 21157-4627
Phone: 1-800-733-3000
Fax: 1-800-659-2436

Insatiable Love 2:

When Broken Hearts Collide

by

Latoya Chandler

Prologue

Dear Diary:

I know I haven't spoken with you in such a long time. I really wish you were a real friend, not me talking to myself about myself. Had you been a real and true friend, you could have told me about my devilish, whorish ways. I don't blame you. I did this to myself. I just wanted to write to you one last time to let you know I'm moving on with my life to try to better myself.

I am going to give my doctor this notebook and the others so he can see the real me, just in case I try to hide something. I didn't realize how messed up I was until I saw someone's life taken right before me. I started out on this last crazy journey of mine on a mission to take back a man who never belonged to me in the first place, only to end up alone and by myself as usual.

What I have learned in the last twenty-four hours is that sex is a physical act that lasts for an hour or so but has the capability to damage your very being for a lifetime. Be careful how you use that deadly weapon between your legs. It can and will kill you in more ways than one.

I'm going on and on as usual, but I find solace in writing down my thoughts. So thank you for listening, my dear friend and diary.
Love Always,
The Woman in Broken Pieces

Chapter One

By Any Means Necessary

Through all of this bickering and fighting with my husband, Bernard blackmails me into memorializing the skeletons of my childhood. Honestly, the way I see it, life has a way of dealing you the same cards over and over. It's just a different scene and characters but pretty much the same scenario. I've never approached the demons of my past, and it appears they've decided to have an all-out intervention with my mind via my darling husband.

I was taught that once our sins are forgiven, they are thrown into the sea of forgetfulness. That includes the sins of our mothers, fathers, and family. All I had to do was forgive them and I would be in a better place with God, cleansed from all I've done, thought, or what was done to me. Right now, I'm starting to wonder how true that is considering the way things have been with Bernard and me. Let's not forget my prison sentence, or bid, I did being married to Braxton.

I don't know where to start. I believe I was a vibrant, energetic child but would find myself in some mischief in one way or another. However, my heartache started long before I was even born. My birth mother wanted to give me up for adoption, but her parents, my biological grandparents, wouldn't allow it. This caused a battle, and my mom eventually gave my grandparents custody of me because they wanted me, and she didn't. They were ultimately deemed unfit. I was with my gradparents for six months after being born with health issues inherited from my mom's drug abuse. Narcotics played a massive part in my mom's life, dictating all her decisions, especially those having to do with loving and accepting me.

I bounced around from foster home to foster home for ten years, which afforded a mix of good and bad experiences. It also left me with a constant sense of abandonment, mistrust, and low self-esteem from growing up not feeling wanted. Fortunately, or not so fortunately for me, I found a foster family who took me in as one of their own on my tenth birthday. They eventually adopted me when I was 14. They were always harder on me than they were with my other adopted siblings. I was told it only appeared that way because I was the oldest of the five children, and more was expected of me.

My foster parents were very rigid in their religious beliefs and made us children obey them—or should I say honor them—or, they told us, our days on earth would be cut short. I usually refused to give into their requests and demands, such as only wearing dresses that went past my knees, because I was made fun of at school. I would steal or borrow my younger sister's pants and would change as soon as I got on the school bus. Because I was older and my body was changing, I was required to hide my body so a man could find me when I came of age and want me for me, not because I was a whore revealing all my body parts.

My foster/adoptive dad, the disciplinarian, caught wind of my rebellious behavior by mysteriously showing up at school during lunch to "see what I was up to." I paid for it severely when I got home from school. Tears threaten my eyes from just reliving the horrific experiences, especially one in particular.

"Sharon, I see you want to be grown and whore around in men's britches," my dad barked.

"No, sir, it was frigid out, so I borrowed Kacey's pants."

"Thou shalt not lie. What commandment are you breaking?" he chastised me, swinging a black leather belt with studs in it, connecting it with the side of my face.

"I am sorry, sir," I screeched through the pain.

"Thou shalt not lie. What commandment are you breaking?"

"The ninth commandment, sir," I howled.

He battered me for what appeared to be days in the most unfriendly and unloving manner with that belt, gifting me with bruises and scars until I believed I was unconscious. After a while, I really did black out. I had marks all over my body and gashes from the studs, so I was forced to stay home from school to hide the contusions and homemade stitches Mommy dearest would inflict or create to close up the deep open wounds the belt had generated.

I eventually ran away from home, not knowing where I was going, which was when I ran into and officially met Braxton, the ladies' man from school. I ended up confessing and telling him about the abuse. After giving him my virginity that evening, I knew he was a godsend the way he made love to me, catering to my body and making me feel wanted and special in a way I had never in my life felt before.

Braxton also allowed me to hide in his grandmother's basement until we came up with a plan B. For that reason alone, I love him the way I do. I feel I owe him for rescuing me from my foster/adoptive parents' abuse. I regret not giving him the one thing he wanted—a child—which is something no other woman has been able to provide him with either. This is what I believed severed our marriage, and ironically, is probably one of the reasons I've grown fond of Latavia. She is allowing his legacy to live on, something no other woman could give him either.

Right now, the one thing missing from my marriage that can and will allow things to flourish between us is a child. I know giving him a son would make things better for us. He just doesn't realize it because he can't get past his own warped belief system. That's why I'm here as his helpmate. My only interference is he always wears a condom when we make love, and there's no way of talking him out of it.

Wait a minute . . . Thank you, God, for the great idea. You see, God will grant you what your heart desires. I just had a thought drop into my spirit. I will puncture holes into all of the condoms in the nightstand with a straight pin so he won't notice them. That way, I can give my husband what no other woman has been able to give him and also have someone to really love me like no other.

Chapter Two

Martinez's Oily Surprise

Thank God for my friend and brother, Carter. I needed that. Now I have to occupy my mind to avoid driving over to where the love of my life, Cola, lives and making an unnecessary scene. Does this woman know or realize how much I love her? We cannot go on with the back-and-forth any longer. I need balance and stability for myself and, most importantly, my Gabby. I think I'm going to bite the bullet and go on over there after getting this place straightened up. We need to talk so I can see where her head is and what she's thinking.

"Oh, shit! Cola, when and how did you get here?" I quiz, startled to see her sitting on my bed as I enter the bedroom.

"I got a little scared, *papi*. I'm sorry. No one has ever treated me the way you do, but I'm here to give us a try and to make it up to you if you'll let me," she baits me.

Mesmerized by her beauty, I almost forget why I was upset or bothered in the first place. Not to mention the scene displayed right before me. She is sitting on top of the bed, which appears to be draped in a shower curtain, wearing only a white T-shirt. Before I can begin to utter a word, she pours some baby oil onto her tits and rubs it in. Her nipples are instantly exposed through the T-shirt, alerting my soldier to stand at full attention. Cola must have noticed she now has my undivided attention. She's pouring it all over herself, pausing at her thighs, massaging the oil in, working her way down to her cleanly shaven kit-kat.

"My candy licker would make you feel better. Let *papi* see how many licks it would take."

"Let me get it nice and wet for you, *papi*," she entices me, painting her clit a creamy shade of white.

She is now removing her shirt, and I'm about to lose my goddamn mind. *I need to be in on this action.* "Is it time for *papi* to come and play?"

Without using words, she declines my admission to the playground, getting on all fours, pointing her immaculate round ass toward me. She pours more baby oil onto her lower back, allowing it to run down her ass, before manipulating it in for me, working her hand in and out of her cheeks and legs.

My heart is racing at record speed. *This is the hottest shit I've ever seen.* "Baby, I can't take it anymore. I want to please you."

Instead of a verbal response, she jiggles her lady parts, gyrating and rubbing herself, summoning me to come join her.

"Lie on your stomach, and keep that ass up," I command, entering her with deep strokes. The feeling of her slippery skin and soaking wet box is better than I've ever imagined it could be. Every single part of her body feels like the inside of her kit-kat—nice and wet. I believe she is the horniest I have ever seen her.

"I want to bounce on it, *papi*," she begs, pouring baby oil on my chest, locking eyes with me, breathing heavy, and licking her lips.

This oil has our bodies sliding against each other and has me going even more. With her feet flat against the bed beside each of my arms, Cola begins some squatting exercises up and down on my Johnson between reaching behind herself to play with the Johnson's twins. I'm not sure if it was the show she gave me, because I usually last longer than this, but I'm about to tap out. I can't hold back any longer.

"Damn, Cola," is all I can utter before my volcano erupts.

This woman sure knows how to get what she wants out of me. *Damn!*

Chapter Three

Bernard Is Out For Self

"Talk to me."

"Yo, Bernard, some shit went down, and Nae is dead," Michael cries.

"Hold up! Slow the fuck down. Dead? As in gone?"

"Are you hard of hearing? You heard what I said!"

"What the fuck happened?"

"Not a hundred percent sure. They're trying to figure it all out, but you know we're on lockdown until further notice. All I know right now is that someone was out to get her and cut her up pretty bad. They cut her fuckin' throat, B."

"Damn, that's fucked up! You seem to be taking this pretty hard, my man. You think you're going to be all right?"

"Man, fuck you!"

"Hello?"

It appears his turned-out ass is in his feelings, hanging up phones and shit. I am a little fucked up that Nae went out like that, but what the fuck was I supposed to do? It was her or me, and I'm not taking the wrap for any of this shit. Michael's nose was so deep in her ass that I couldn't risk it. I did what was necessary. I feel bad. She got caught up in something she had no business in from the gate.

I think I'll take this time to go give my boy a visit. *I haven't seen him in a minute,* I ponder, driving in the direction of the hospital. I've been trying to give him a minute to get his mental straight and deal with Latavia's ass.

"Hey, D! What's up, partner? You're looking good, my man."

"I can't call it, Nard. Where's your ass been?"

"Dealing with Sharon's crazy ass and giving you time, you know?"

"So now you know what I need?"

"Man, I'm just looking out for you as usual."

"Go ahead with that. So what's new?"

"Not a damn thing. Oh, yeah, I ran into your old flame, D."

"Who?"

"Nicole's trifling ass."

"Is that right? It looks like she's running into everyone these days."

"Why you say that?"

"She came up here talking nonsense. Speaking of that, why the fuck did you tell her where to find me?"

"It wasn't like that, D. I didn't give her specifics. She must have figured that shit out."

"I shouldn't have been on your lips in a conversation with that trick, real talk."

"Why are you upset? You still crushing on her, D?" he taunts.

"Shut the fuck up, Nard. I have a woman. I'm good."

"So what's up? What did she want?"

"She's up to no good, coming up here out of the blue on some bullshit. Then Martinez comes up here to visit the following day all upset about his old lady, who happens to be Nicole!"

"Get the fuck out of here! It can't be the same Nicole."

"I kid you not. He showed me a picture of her."

"That's some fucked-up shit."

"How so? What she and I had has been long gone. That's Martinez's headache, not mine."

"You're right about that shit."

Damn! How the hell did Nicole just happen to forget to mention she's fucking Martinez too? That's some bullshit! She's just fucking through all of us? What? She thinks we wouldn't catch on? We do this shit for a living. It's just unfortunate for Martinez's dumb ass because he's caught the fuck up not knowing his bitch is a ho. I'm not going to alert him of it either. As long as she's keeping my dick hard, we're good.

Chapter Four

Darnell Wants To Fix Things

"Hello, Darnell's room."

"Darnell?"

"Yes, Latavia, what's wrong? Why are you crying?"

"She's gone, and it's all my fault."

"Who's gone, baby? Please calm down and talk to me."

"Nae is gone, Darnell, and it's all my fault."

"What do you mean, gone? She escaped from prison?"

"No, one of those dyke bitches killed her."

"I am so sorry, baby. Let me make a couple of phone calls and see what I can find out. How did you hear about it? Was it on the news?"

"Some woman administrator from the Department of Corrections called me. She said Nae had me listed as her next of kin."

"Fuck, Latavia! This should not have gone down like this. Please try to calm down, baby. I'm going to try to make a few calls and call you right back."

"Okay, Darnell, I love you so much, and I'm sorry."

"I love you more."

This shit is crazy as hell. I've never wished death on ol' girl. I couldn't believe she was locked up in the first place, and now she's dead?

I try calling Nard's ass twice after hanging up with Latavia, and I keep going straight to voicemail. Right now, this isn't what Latavia needs. She can't handle any more heartache. To make matters worse, I'm locked up in this fucking place and can't be there for my wife when she needs me to be. I have to figure out how I can get a pass or something, but Bernard's ass is nowhere to be found. Fuck! She's pregnant and in no condition to make funeral arrangements alone. I have to fix this. Hell, I can't bring Nae back. What am I going to do? Fuck! Let me calm my ass down to try to process this shit.

Fuck!

Chapter Five

Latavia Blames Herself

Words cannot express or describe what I am feeling right now. Everyone I've ever loved has been stripped from me. BK and Nae are dead and Darnell is locked up in a hospital because I was dumb and not thinking. All of this is my fault. Had I not run out of the house like a freaking idiot, none of this would be going on, and I wouldn't be sitting here crying all alone with no one.

Oh, God! My stomach is cramping. I'm stressing this baby now. "Lord, please help me," I yelp, grabbing my midsection as a sharp pain shoots through me. *Let me try to relax my mind and get myself together,* I think, reaching for my cell to call the only person I have right about now.

"Hey, Sharon. I am glad you answered."

"You don't sound like yourself, Latavia. Are you all right?"

"No, I am not. Nae's gone," I weep.

"I know. Have you tried to go see her to try to patch things up? It's just a suggestion. I just know how close you two were."

"It's a little too late for that."

"No, it's never too late. I'm sure she could use a friend right now."

"Well, I haven't been remotely close to that, and now she's dead."

"What are you saying, Latavia? How? Oh, my goodness."

"I got a call not too long ago from the Department of Corrections, or whatever they're called, and they informed me she's gone, or 'has expired,' as they put it."

"Jesus, we need you right now! I am going to come over. You're definitely not in any condition to be alone right now. I won't take no for an answer."

"Thank you. I'm really afraid to be alone right now, and these pains I'm having are making me nervous."

"Say no more. As soon as Bernard gets in, I will get him settled and come right over."

"Thank you so much, Sharon."

"No problem at all. Just try to sit down and relax. I know—it's easier said than done."

Chapter Six

Dear Diary

Dear Diary:
Hey, you. I know it's been a couple of minutes since we've spoken, and so much has happened. For starters, my papi had a romantic evening planned, which I caught wind of after speaking to Granny. You know the old lady can't hold water. Anyway, he arranged for a limo to pick me up at his place and take me to the spa, which was so needed. It gave me time to think and put two and two together. I knew good and well that if I went back to that house, he would have been on some Boyz II Men tip on bended knee, and marriage was never part of the plan. Don't get me wrong, I do care for him and never expected to fall for him, but I did. It's just unfortunate my heart, mind, body, and soul belong to you-know-who. Yes, before you ask, I still can't say his name without tearing up.

Back to the matter at hand. I had to think fast after bailing out on my papi, so you know I did what I do best—I threw this sweet, fat, hypnotizing dick trap on him, and he's even more open than he was before. You should have seen me. I put on a show, and all it took was a shower curtain, baby oil, and one of his white tees. Talk about sexing on a budget. I can teach you some shit. Yeah, I know I am crazy as hell, but that's why you love me the way you do.

Oh, yeah, before I forget, I went to try to visit you-know-who again, and they wouldn't even let me in. They said I don't have clearance, and I'm not on the visiting list, and if I come back, they will call the authorities and have me arrested. Ain't that some shit? I read between the lines, and the bottom line is he wants to be loyal to that tramp of his. Seeing me or being around me would abort that dedication of his. That just excites me even more, and now I am on to plan B, C, D, and E, whatever they are. So with that, my friend, I'm going to call it a night. My papi will be back from his shower any minute, and I need to rock his ass to sleep.

Love Always,
The Real Mrs. Carter aka Nikki the Sex Freak

Chapter Seven

Sharon Feels Latavia's Pain

I cannot imagine what's possibly going through that poor woman's mind. This is god-awful. "Lord, I pray you send angels to encamp around Latavia to comfort and protect her mind. Amen."

Why today of all days did Bernard decide to come home late? I really want to get over to Latavia's. She really shouldn't be alone right now in her condition. This is way too much for her to handle, or anyone to handle for that matter. If I believed in luck, I'd say she had the worst luck anyone could ask for.

"Get dressed, young lady. I made dinner plans for us," Bernard notifies me, walking through the door in an exceptionally good mood.

"Hello to you, handsome. I see someone's in a very good mood this evening."

"Why shouldn't I be?"

"It's just good to see you this way, but can we postpone dinner? I want to go see about Latavia. She's all alone over there, dealing with all of this. I'm sure you heard about Nariah, right?"

"Yes, I did, and why the fuck is that your concern? That's Latavia's problem, not yours. Your problem is me. So get your ass together and don't ruin my evening."

"Bernard, you can't be this coldhearted. The woman is dead, and Latavia is all by herself. She has no one. We can't just leave her by herself."

"The bitch was born alone. She will be A-okay if she spends a little more time alone. Now I'm asking you nicely, please get your ass ready. Better yet, wear what you have on and let's go."

"Please give me a minute to freshen up. I'll meet you in the car in less than five minutes."

"You better not have me out there waiting too long for your ass either."

"I promise I'll be right out.

"Dear God, what am I going to do with this man? He is so set in his ways and wants me all to himself. I guess I got what I prayed for, so I can't complain, but I have to be able to have friends. My life cannot center solely on him. Not to mention, this woman is all alone, and it breaks my heart just thinking about it. I'm going to call her real quick to let her know I'll be over in the morning after I see Bernard off to work. Better yet, I'll text her because hearing the sadness in her voice will tear me to pieces right now, and I need to be whole to deal with this husband of mine. Lord, I thank you for him, but he is a piece of work."

To Latavia: I apologize, but I can't get over there this evening. Bernard made plans without me knowing, and I can't get out of them. I'll come by in the morning. Again, I do apologize.

From Latavia: I understand, Sharon. I kind of dozed off a little. I'm going to try to get some rest. I'll see you in the morning.

To Latavia: Great. See you then, and I'm praying for you.

I am so glad that worked out. Now let me get to this car before he turns into that ugly person I didn't marry and fall in love with.

Chapter Eight

Martinez's Visit With Granny

Cola has dinner plans with friends this evening. I am going to take Gabby out to dinner and to visit Granny. In fact, I think I'll go by Granny's first. I'm most certain she's cooked enough for an army. That old lady loves to cook, and I love to eat—a match made in heaven if you ask me. She prepares meals as if she were catering for an army. Granny says, "You never know when someone's going to stop by on an empty stomach, so I have to stay prepared. I can't have my babies going home with their stomach's crying." Everyone's her baby. God knows I have grown extremely fond of that woman.

"Hey, princess. What do you think about going over to Granny's for dinner tonight?"

"Can I go and get my baby first, Papa? I want to show Granny her new dress."

"Of course you can, princess."

"I'm ready, Papa," Gabby yells, running down the hall past me to the front door.

It just amazes me how much my princess loves Granny, and how she treats Gabby as if she is her blood grand-child. The best thing that has happened to me is meeting Cola. Had I not met the woman of my dreams, I would not have been afforded the honor and privilege of meeting the best grandmother a kid and her dad could ask for.

"We are all set, little lady. Are you sure you have everything?" I ask before pulling the car out of the driveway.

"No, Papa, you're forgetting something."

"What's that, princess?"

"It's 'House Party' time," she sang.

"How could I forget our road music?" I mumble, adjusting the CD changer to the first track on the infamous Dan Zanes and Friends *House Party* CD. "God, do I hate this song, but anything for my Gabby," I mope.

"Papa, you're not singing."

"I'm right here with you, Gabby," I reply as I begin to chime in on the second verse to sing along with her.

> *Oh, come on in the kitchen*
> *It's filling up with food*
> *There's music in the hallway*
> *Everybody's in the mood*
> *Ring ring doorbell ring*
> *It's house party time (house party time)*
> *House party time (house party time)*

"Perfect timing, Papa. Every time we get to the 'It's party time' part of the song, we're at Granny's house," she screams. She jumps out of the car and runs up the walkway into the arms of her Granny, who happens to be standing in her doorway awaiting our arrival.

This old lady must have magical powers along with all the other great attributes she possesses. Each and every time we visit, with or without notice, she's always standing outside or in the doorway to greet us. Somewhat amazing if you ask me, and Gabby timing the lyrics to the song to how long it takes to get here is near genius. She is a police officer in the making, and she doesn't even know it yet.

"What are you out there doing, Marty? Come on inside and get some food in your belly," Granny summons me.

She tickles me when she calls me Marty, but I love it at the same time. "Yes, ma'am, coming right in."

"How are you doing, sweetie?"

"I am great, Granny, and yourself?" I ask, greeting her with a kiss to the cheek.

"Better now that my grandbaby is here."

"What am I, chopped liver?"

"Hush now, Marty. Granny has more than enough love to give to all my babies, including you," she humors me.

"It smells good in here as usual. What's on the menu?"

"Not too much, baby, just a little something I threw together. Some cornbread, black-eyed peas, fried chicken, green beans, potato salad, and a German chocolate cake. Oh, and some ice cream if you eat all your food."

"Lord have mercy, Granny. I think I'm in love."

"Hush now. Go and get yourself freshened up while me and my grandbaby get your plate together."

If I weren't in love with Cola, I promise I would marry Granny. She sure knows how to make a man feel loved, feeding me like this and loving my Gabby the way she does.

"What's on your mind, Marty? Come on in here before your food gets cold, baby."

"Nothing much. I just wanted to come see the best granny in the world and get a nice, home-cooked meal."

"Nicole starving you over there, boy?"

"No, ma'am. She went out with friends this evening."

"Well, how did your romantic evening go?"

"Not as planned, but it was good overall."

"Marty, baby, I know Nicole is my grandbaby, but I think you need to focus more on you and Gabby. I can tell you think her shit doesn't stink, but when you turn around, the roses smell like boo-boo, son."

"What are you trying to say, Granny?"

"Love her, Marty, but don't lose yourself while loving her. Every vagina that glitters ain't gold, son."

Chapter Nine

Bernard Is In A Good Mood

Things went according to plan. I picked up Nae's little spy cam or fuck recorder and destroyed all of the existing evidence. Now I can relax and not worry about shit. I am in such a great mood, I didn't even trip on Nicole about fucking Martinez when I spoke with her. I even went ahead and made reservations for Sharon and me to go out to Don Pepe's for dinner. I have a little surprise for her as well. If she doesn't hurry her ass up out of that house, she's going to upset me and ruin my mood. She has a lot of damn nerve trying to cancel my plans to go and rescue Latavia's ass. That shit ain't got nothing to do with us. That's her problem. Everyone is always jumping for her pathetic ass. Not on my watch you won't.

"What the hell were you doing in there?" I bark as Sharon finally gets her ass in the car.

"I had to change my top, Bernard. Where are we going anyway?"

"Don Pepe's, and I have a surprise for you when we get there."

"Really, baby? What is it?"

"Calm yourself down. You will see as soon as we get there."

"I am so excited, baby."

"You should be."

"Thank you so much, baby. I'm so happy to see God has answered my prayers and things are getting back on track with us."

It looks like my surprise beat us here, I think, noticing Nicole's car as we pull in.

"Okay, we're here. Where's my surprise?"

"Inside. Now let's go."

As we enter Don Pepe's, I see Nicole sitting in the back by the fireplace, and my shit gets stiff as soon as I lay eyes on her sexy ass.

"Why is she here, Bernard?"

"She's part of my surprise. We're going to have dinner, and I got us a nice suite at the Marriott as well."

"I am not doing this again. I'll be in the car."

"Carry your ass to the car then. Nicole and I will enjoy dinner without your bipolar ass. I'm in a good mood, and you're fucking it up."

"Maybe I should go," Nicole interjects.

"That's a great idea," Sharon rebuts.

"No one's going anywhere. Sharon, sit your ass down and be quiet before you make a scene," I snarl through clenched teeth.

"I am not staying. I will catch a taxi back to the house. Enjoy your evening, because I refuse to do this again. I love you but not that much, my love," she whimpers.

Chapter Ten

Darnell To The Rescue

The Man Upstairs looked out for a brother. I was granted a two-week leave from the psychiatric ward to be there for Latavia and assist her with whatever she needs me to do. I had to get clearance from my physician and treatment team, which was a piece of cake, along with telling a little white lie, recognizing Nariah as my sister. After that, it was smooth sailing. My favorite friend and favorite judge, Judge Clemmons, approved my leave request. Now all I need is for Martinez or Nard to get back with me so one of them can pick me up. I have to have a police escort out of here, and Judge Clemmons left it up to me to make that happen. Small perk for being a former dedicated police officer, I'm assuming.

"Oh, shit, Martinez, I just called you not too long ago. What brings you here?"

"I got your message, man. I'm so sorry to hear about Nariah. I was with Gabby visiting Granny, so I left her there and came right over when I heard the message."

"Good looking, my man. I couldn't catch up with Bernard."

"It's cool. The front desk already filled me in and had me sign my life away, so as soon as the doc comes in here to read you your rights, we will be on our way."

"Read me my rights? Look who brought jokes," I chuckle.

"You know how it is, considering the situation."

"Yes, you are right. I am so fucked up over all of this. Latavia has no one right now. I should have been there with her when she received that call."

"Man, don't beat yourself up over it. You will be there within an hour or so. I am sure she'll be relieved when she sees you now."

Chapter Eleven

Latavia Is In The Closet

I don't know why I thought I would be able to sleep.
Every noise in this place startles me, and for the first time
in a long time, I'm afraid to be in this house alone. When
I was younger and afraid, I would sleep in my closet to
try to hide from my father and the outside world. That
was my secret place to shield myself from everything and
everyone. I discovered that the smothering dirty laundry,
hanging clothes, and shoes burying me in darkness was
the easiest way for me to escape reality and relax, and
that's why I find myself as a grown, pregnant woman
squished lying on the floor of my bedroom closet with a
pillow and blanket.

I'm not crazy, but it sounds like someone's here.
Damn it, I forgot to change the locks. Please don't let
Bernard come in here and bother me. I don't have the
energy or strength to deal with him right now. I just can't
take anything else at this moment in my life.

"Latavia, where are you?" a voice that sounds like
Darnell's calls from down the hall.

"Oh, my God, I have lost my mind."

"Where the fuck can she be?"

Maybe I am dreaming, because Darnell's voice is closer and is now in the bedroom. "I'm definitely going to see a doctor in the morning. There is no way in hell I'm going to be pregnant in a straitjacket. I have officially lost my mind," I chuckle.

"Latavia, what the hell are you doing in here?" Darnell asks, puzzled, opening the closet door to see me balled up into a knot on the floor.

"Darnell, how did you get out?" I weep as he helps me up off the floor.

"Temporary release to be here for you. The Man Upstairs knew you needed me. Why the fuck are you in the closet?"

"That's my safe place. I'm scared, Darnell. Everything I touch and love gets destroyed or dies."

"I am here now, beautiful. You are not alone, and you didn't destroy anything."

"Nae is gone because of me and so is . . . never mind."

"It is not your fault. Please come and lie down. I'll hold you until you fall asleep. You can scream, cry, and take it all out on me if you need to. I'm here now, Latavia."

"I'm going to be on my way, Darnell," Martinez interrupts from down the hall.

"Thanks, man. I'll get with you in the morning."

"Take your time, and, Latavia, I am so sorry for your loss."

"Thank you, Martinez."

Chapter Twelve

Sharon Has No Place To Go

"There isn't a chance in hell I'm doing this with Bernard again. How could he do this to me again?" I sob, breaking down. I'm going to pull myself together, wait for this taxi to take me over to Latavia's, and deal with that husband of mine another time. He can't continue to treat me any kind of way. What I don't understand is why that woman, Nicole, is okay with all of this. What kind of woman enjoys being the other person? Maybe she's a prostitute and he's paying her. Well, I hope he gets his money's worth without me, because I am sick of this crazy mess.

I really hope Latavia doesn't mind me just showing up when I originally said I would come by in the morning. She didn't pick up when I phoned, so I'm assuming she's asleep. I really hate to wake her, but I have no place else to go. I guess it's going to be what it is, because I'm here now.

The doorbell chimes, alerting Latavia of her visitor, who happens to be me.

"Who is it?" a male voice whispers in an aggressive tone.

"It's Sharon," I shout back through the door.

"Hey, Sharon. Latavia is resting. Can I help you with something?" Darnell asks as he opens the door.

Caught off guard, I reply, "Yes, Latavia called earlier and informed me about Nariah and didn't want to be alone. I was supposed to come in the morning, but as luck would have it, I had an unbecoming change of plans."

"Pardon my manners. Please come in."

Well, well, well. The man who busted into the hotel room and killed my Braxton is looking magically delicious. *Get thee behind me, Satan. I belong to Bernard,* I silently rebuke. I have to admit, he looks a lot better than that sweaty, malnourished man I met months back. He is a very attractive dark-skinned man, I must say. There's no sin in giving honor where honor is due, and this man is fine.

"I do apologize for imposing. I just don't have any other place to go."

"You and my boy good?"

"We had a fight. Do you mind if I crash on your sofa for a couple of days to get my head together? I know this is bad timing, but I just don't have any other place to go right now."

"This is ironic as hell, but give me a minute to make sure it's fine with my wife first."

He's 100 percent correct about that. This is quite paradoxical. I set out to destroy this woman, and now I need her friendship more than she knows. Like the Bible says, it was meant for evil, but it works together for our good, and we are witnesses of that at this point in time.

Chapter Thirteen

Martinez's Eye-Opener

Seeing the agony in Carter's face when he heard his wife in the closet and opened the door to see her lying on the floor was a sight I wish I hadn't seen. That messed me up something bad and tugged at my heartstrings. I had to back my way out of the room down the steps to allow them privacy. This is by far one heartache I can't imagine dealing with. The two of them do love one another, and I can see that myself. Bad choices put a roadblock in the way of their love.

All of this is just an eye-opener for me, telling me to give Cola the time she needs and not to rush things. I also heard Granny loud and clear and read between the lines of our conversation. In other words, she thinks that I'm so whipped and at the mercy of her high-maintenance granddaughter and that I'm blinded by her penis sheath. Little does she know, it's much more than sex for me. I love Cola. I know she isn't ready to take it further, so I'm going to bear with her and give her the time she needs.

One thing is for sure, I will focus more on Gabby's well-being. I've seen a lot of messed-up women, including her mother. I don't want my princess to grow up in a fucked-up headspace like that. Little girls need their daddies as well as their mommies. I just hope Cola comes around sooner rather than later so we can give Gabby the stability she needs.

Jessica must have forgotten she has a child, because we have yet to hear a word out of her. To think I fell in love with that woman, married her, and lay down with her. Never in a million years would I have thought things would have spiraled out of control like that between her and me. I am just glad it happened when it did, while Gabby is young. I still have time to show her the right way, and I rescued her before Jessica's ass ruined her.

Chapter Fourteen

Bernard Is Furious

"I am so upset I can't even enjoy my meal. I can't believe she walked her ass up out of here and disrespected me like that."

"B, chill out. Let her calm down. You can't just spring me on women. They can't handle it. I'm a threat to them, so you have to understand. Hell, I do."

"Nicole, shut the fuck up please."

"What you aren't going to do is talk to me any kind of way. I'm not your wife."

"No, you're the cunt who's fucked through the entire NYPD. I pulled your card. What? You thought no one was going to find out?"

"Hold up, you knew about me and your boy from the jump, so don't go catching feelings like your wife."

"Martinez was a surprise, but if you fucked my boy over, you're liable to do anything. Shit, you're fucking me with and without my wife, so no shock here."

"Excuse me? What are you talking about?"

"Don't play dumb. You know what the fuck I'm talking about."

"Whatever, B."

"Now it's whatever. You don't have much to say now, I see. What? Now all of a sudden cat got your tongue?"

"I'm leaving. You will not disrespect me like this."

"You're a disrespect to your own nasty self, bitch," I taunt, throwing my drink in her face before excusing myself from the table.

She wanted a scene, and that's just what she got. I am sick of these broads thinking they have the upper hand. I don't need Nicole's nasty ass, even though she rides this dick like a thoroughbred. I will just have to train Sharon's ass how to ride it correctly after I set her ass straight. There isn't a chance in hell I'm going to allow a wife of mine to just walk out on me, embarrassing me, when I was going out of my way to be good to her. Fuck that!

Shit, I must be on fire. I got home that fast. "Sharon, bring your ass down here!" I demand, slamming the door behind me.

"You don't hear me talking to you, woman?" I check every room in the house, and this bitch is nowhere to be found. She'd better not be with Latavia. I specifically told her to mind her business. I'm about to head over there to find out. That's her ass if she's there.

Damn, I'm breaking records today. How the hell did I get here this fast? I'm getting soft, letting this woman get me upset like this.

"Latavia, open this fuckin' door! I know Sharon's in there!"

"Yo, B, be easy banging on the door like that, and calm the fuck down!" my boy reprimands, opening the door.

"My bad, D. When the fuck you get out?"

"That's not important right now. I need you to calm down. You have this woman over here trembling because you're acting like the Incredible Hulk for nothing."

"I'm going to calm down, but this has nothing to do with you, D, so fall back, man."

"When you brought it to my doorstep, you involved me, and I don't feel comfortable letting Sharon leave with you in the state you're in."

"Worry about your wife, and let me handle mine, D. You're my boy and all, but this is none of your business."

"I'm not leaving with you, Bernard," Sharon screams from behind D.

"Sharon, don't get over here and lose your mind pulling that shit Latavia pulls on D. I'm not the one."

"What the fuck you mean by that, B? You'd better go before this escalates into something your ass can't cash. I'm not these women. I will fuck you up for disrespecting me, my house, and my wife."

"I will deal with you later, D. Sharon, bring your ass on."

"I'm not going anywhere. Go back to Ni—" was all she got out before I reached around my boy and slapped blood from her mouth.

"Nard, get the fuck out of my house!" D barks, grabbing me by my shirt and shoving me back out the door.

"Fuck you and that bitch. I don't need any of your asses."

Chapter Fifteen

Darnell Grants Latavia's Wish

"Sharon, what the fuck is up with him? Are you okay? Shit, let me go get you something for your mouth."

"I am so sorry to bring this mess to your house and get you involved. I will get a hotel room. I am truly sorry."

"You will not do anything of the sort," Latavia asserted.

"Baby girl, I was hoping you slept through this bullshit."

"It appears sleep is not on my horizon."

"Latavia, I am truly sorry for bringing my mess to your house. This is the last thing you need."

"Sharon, you did nothing wrong. It's okay. Just make yourself comfortable and try to get some rest. We can talk in the morning."

"Baby girl, you're the one who's supposed to be resting. Let's get you back in bed."

"It feels so good having you home, baby," she whimpers, burying her head in my chest as we retreat upstairs.

Why the hell, now of all times, is my Jimmy up looking for action? Now is not the time, but my shit is growing by the minute. That's what this woman does to me. I don't think she has any idea how much I'm in love with everything about her.

"It looks like someone wants to come out and play."

"I will be all right, Latavia. This is the wrong time to be thinking about making love to you."

"Baby, just let me take care of you, please? Let me put my mouth on it just the way you like it, daddy. Fuck my mouth, baby."

"Damn, girl, stop saying that shit. You got me solid as a rock right about now."

I love when she talks that shit. As a man, I have to comply and give her what she's asking for. Fuck my mouth, she beckoned? I have to be a man about it and grant her wish. In other words, fuck her mouth until her other lips cum.

"Just the way I like it, daddy."

Sitting up on the bed, she pulls me closer to her, lifting my shirt as she places soft, wet kisses on my stomach—her indirect signal for me to remove my shirt. As I follow her lead and makes sure my shirt vanishes, she continues greeting my abdomen with her lips as she unbuckles and unzips my trousers, allowing them to collapse at my feet.

"There's the dark chocolate momma's been craving." She drools.

Holding my masterpiece by the base, she begins licking it like an ice cream cone. A chocolate one with rainbow sprinkles to be exact—her favorite. Her tongue thrashes it from the base upward, switching sides. She flicks her miracle-working tongue back and forth across my corona.

"Shit, baby girl, I missed those juicy lips of yours—both sets."

Keeping herself aroused, she takes my right hand and traces her swollen clit with her fingers, finding pleasure with her own touch.

"Let me help you with that. Sit that sweet stuff on daddy's face."

"Babe, I want to please you."

"Stop talking. A brother has to eat, too. Now come have a seat and let daddy suck that creamy stuff out of your chocolate vault."

Out of obedience, she sits her leaking faucet on my face with her ass facing me so she can continue feasting on her chocolate. Grabbing my third leg with her hands, Latavia proceeds to stroke it as she works on the tip with her tongue and lips, making sure to stimulate the boys in between.

"Oh, my God! Darnell, that feels so good."

It is becoming a difficult task for her to ensure I give her the best I've got because I am slaughtering her birth canal with every part of my mouth. "This is about him. I can't slack," she moans, moving her tongue in circles on my shit, establishing a swirl motion and using her hands in between to give her jaws a small break before going in for the kill. With that being said, she turns her mouth into an automatic Hoover, sucking and slurping on her Mr. Goodbar until every nut evaporates down her throat.

Chapter Sixteen

Sharon Is Resentful

The soft but masculine moans cascading down the stairs rally me to follow their impression overhead to where I am now planted outside of Darnell and Latavia's bedroom door. They neglected to shut it all the way, as if they wanted to put on a show for me. The devil is really busy and has seized my body. I want to walk myself back down the stairs, but I'm stuck. The only thing that manages to move are my hands as they travel to my southern region.

I don't know what it is, but the sounds coming from his mouth are igniting a fire in my sacred place—that is, until my eyes land on his wife. This woman has it all: a man who loves her dirty drawers, and she's pregnant by the man whose dirty drawers I am in love with. It isn't fair.

I'm the God-fearing woman, I walk according to the Word, and yet my life is a living hell. Yes, the Bible says God sends rain on the just as well as the unjust, but it didn't say anything about Satan's spawn. When is it my turn to be happy? When will God rain on me? Why do I have to continue to suffer with a husband who doesn't love or care for me the way I do him, the same husband who wants to purchase a Baby Alive doll for me instead of affording me the honor and privilege of giving birth? Yet this ungrateful woman gets knocked up by another man, and he still loves her unconditionally. She really doesn't deserve him. I deserve to have Darnell, not her. It's really unfair to me. It really is.

"Lord, I ask you to forgive me for my thoughts and actions this evening. I know it's not by chance you have me here with the both of them. Please reveal to me what it is you want me to see, do, and change. Amen!"

Chapter Seventeen

Nicole's Daddy Issues

I don't know what the hell crawled up Nard's ass for him to think it was completely fine for him to talk to me anyway he pleased and toss his drink in my face. I am not that basket-case wife of his. I had to play it cool because it appears he's keeping my secret about my *papi.* How the hell did he find out anyway? I must have put it on him so good that he's now following me around. That's the only way he could have found out.

My *papi* is very private. He keeps his personal life home, and I reiterated that to him so I don't get caught out there. It's been a year we've been doing this dating thing, so I know he's not running his mouth. Either way, I'll play it cool with Nard. I don't want to mess that up either, because he definitely knows how to dig my guts out, and that is the only reason I continue to deal with him.

My trust for the male species is at an all-time low, and it has been since I was a teenage girl. That seed was planted when I became old enough to ask questions such as, "Why does my dad send money every week instead of bringing himself to see and spend time with me?" Every Saturday morning when the mail carrier arrived, Mommy was beyond ecstatic to announce, "Look what your daddy sent for you, Nikki." My naive, loving, robotic mother said he worked on the road as a truck driver, and when he got the opportunity to come home, it was always late in the evening, and he left before the sun rose. Now that I think about it, Mommy sounded like a booty call.

I fell for that bogus story until I was around 15 or 16 years of age. I couldn't fathom how my mother could be engaged forever with no man in sight to claim her. My dad must have been a hell of a man to be kept a secret, because I never saw him, and neither did anyone else in the family.

Granny would say, "Mommy's in love with the invisible man or a married man," and she would put money on it that it was a married man her dumb ass was engaged to. Well, Granny was on the money with that one. I decided to stay up one of the evenings I knew he was due to come by. Like clockwork, Mommy would go out of her way cleaning the house as if we were having an inspection, and everything would be spotless. She would cook on these particular evenings the way Granny does, when on any other day it would be takeout or TV dinners for us. I caught on quickly and decided that the next time Mommy was in a cleaning and cooking mood, I would stay up to try to get a glimpse of, or finally meet, my daddy.

Precisely at nine, Mommy retired to her room. I followed suit to mine, turned the lights out so it looked like I was going to bed, and waited for the guest of the night to arrive. To my surprise, I didn't have to wait long. Three hours later, I could hear her walking downstairs, and not too long after, a male voice was heard. That was my cue to meet the mystery man also known as my father.

"Sorry, Mommy, I didn't know you had company. My bad," I fibbed, running smack-dab into her and the mystery man as they reached the top of the stairs.

"I guess it's time you met your father. Nikki, this is Walter, your dad. Walter, this is your angel, Nicole."

"Good to meet you, baby girl," the strange man now known as my father angrily greeted me.

I thought the first time meeting my dad, who appears to love his work more than his only daughter, would be the best day of my life. News flash: it was the opposite. For one, he looked at me with disappointment in his eyes, which turned into a lustful stare. The look the boys in school gave me was the same way my dad looked at me. That made my skin crawl. Our introduction was as far as it went. He and Mommy went straight into her room. That was when all hell broke loose.

"I told you to make sure your fast-ass daughter was asleep."

"Walter, she's sixteen now. Don't you think it's long overdue you meet and spend time with our daughter? And for the record, she is not fast."

"Don't get beside yourself slick talking me. You know I have no problem whatsoever going upside your head."

"I'm sorry, honey, but we can't go on like this forever. You told me your divorce would be final I don't know how many years ago, and nothing's changed."

"What the fuck did I tell you about questioning me?" he howled before slapping Mommy clear across the room.

Mommy was five feet four inches and 145 pounds soaking wet. When I heard my sperm donor enraged, I eased my way toward the room and heard everything through the door. I was too afraid to go into the room although I wanted to help Mommy when I heard the coward pummeling blow after blow on her like she was a punching bag or he was some dude off the streets. The hate for him and all men that manifested that night is indescribable.

That was the first and last time I laid eyes on the deadbeat. Mommy started spending time out of the house on her visitation days after the beating. I think, now that I'm older, I need to hire someone to look into his where-abouts, because I need to deal with this once and for all. I'll start off with Granny to see if she has any information on him, considering all I have is the first name of my own father. Sad but true. I'm not going to leave this earth like Mommy did from a broken heart. No man will ever get so close to me that I go to sleep one night after suffering a bout of depression and never wake back up. Not going to happen.

Chapter Eighteen

Bernard Is Not Having It

Sharon's done lost her way. She has been hanging around Latavia a little too much, talking to me like she's crazy. I should have knocked her in her mouth instead of slapping her ass. Now D has his simpleton monkey ass involved when this doesn't have shit to do with him. That's my man, a hundred grand, but I'm going to hold my own, and shit's going to be what it is at the end of the day. I gave him space with Latavia when I felt he should have stepped out on her or left, but I can't get the same respect in return.

I am going to give Sharon two to three days tops to get her shit together and carry her ass back home before I replace her and put her shit out. She's got me fucked up playing these games. My mom's pulled shit like this on my pops. There isn't a chance in hell I'm going to allow history to repeat itself or raise its funky-ass head on me. I'm canceling that shit from the gate.

Moms didn't want kids, but she had us to appease Pops. She said no one had ever loved her growing up. She didn't have time to be trying to love more people than herself and Pops. My twin sister died at birth, so it was just me. Moms couldn't even get that shit right.

Moms would say that can't no one love her better than herself now that she knew who she was. She would say that shit all the time arguing with Pops. She didn't conceal her feelings when I was around either.

Pops loved me and tried to make up for that shit. It didn't work, because she left our asses high and dry. I will never forget being awakened by Pops whimpering as he read the letter she'd penned before vanishing in the night. The crazy shit about it is to this day she has never come back to check on me or reconcile things with Pops. I'm a grown-ass man, and the last time I saw Moms, I was 10 years old. Ain't that about a bitch?

That's some shit, now that I think about it. If Sharon thinks I'm going to knock her up so she can disappear on me and my seed, I'm not going to even entertain or set myself up for that. I'll pass. We're good just the way we are. Why try to fix something that isn't broke?

Chapter Nineteen

Darnell's Houseguest

Last night reminded me of one of the reasons why Latavia has my nose wide open. That was some shit. She worked the hell out of my joint. Now she's got me in the kitchen, slaving over a hot stove, making breakfast. Everything feels like it used to before our worlds collided. I will make sure to prepare enough food for our houseguest. Speaking of her, I hope we weren't too loud and she didn't hear us. Hell, she's grown and knows how it is. She'll be all right if she did. Sharon isn't a bad-looking woman. She just looks stressed the fuck out. B must be driving her crazy. He was dead-ass wrong for putting his hands on her, real talk. I'm going to give him some breathing room, but I plan on checking him on that and for disrespecting my place.

"Good morning, Darnell. Would you like some help?" Sharon volunteers, brushing up against me.

I hope I'm taking that little gesture the wrong way, but there is more than enough room in this kitchen, so that is alarming.

"No, thank you. I got it. You can have a seat and make yourself comfortable at the table. Latavia should be coming down any minute," I reply, my back still facing her. I'm not trying to give her any inclinations or ideas if that's what she's looking for.

I guess I'm still a little paranoid after that fiasco with Nariah and all the shit that went down. Let me chill and get my mind right. Mona, their assistant, or the real owner of Elite, is supposed to be coming through this afternoon to help Latavia with the arrangements for Nariah's homegoing service. My wife gets upset when I acknowledge Mona as the real owner, but the way I see it, she runs that place and never skips a beat. Shit, with everything that's transpired within the last six months to a year, Latavia is blessed to still have a company. I bet she can't even recall the last time she stepped into her own office. With that, I rest my case. Mona is a blessing to Elite, and I'm grateful to her for holding my wife down the way she does.

Chapter Twenty

Latavia Is Grief-Stricken

It felt like old times last night. I love having Darnell back around. I didn't realize how much I really missed him. Although I'm dreading today, I feel all right about it because he's here with me. Thank God for Mona. I don't know what I would do without her. She knows me, Nae, and Elite like the back of her hand. Her dedication and loyalty are unheard of. When she didn't hear from me or Nae, she continued to carry on with things without a second thought. Once things have settled down a bit, and I'm in the right state of mind to carry out my day-to-day functions with Elite properly, I'm going to offer her a position as a partner. It's only right. The hard part will be finding another one of her to replace her.

Whatever Darnell is down there cooking is dispersing an aroma that is petitioning me to get my butt downstairs quick, fast, and in a hurry. I am starving. I haven't had an appetite in weeks, but as soon as my love comes home, my greedy butt is ready to get my grub on. God in heaven knows how much I love that man. I still feel like a complete idiot for stepping out on him, calling myself giving up on him and my marriage. He is a rare breed to love me past all of that and still accept me and this baby.

Let me pull myself together before the sprinkler system in my face turns on. I need to put something in my belly before Mona arrives.

"Good morning, sleepyhead," I say. "How did you sleep, Sharon? Forgive me, I almost forgot you were down here."

"I couldn't sleep at all, just too much on my mind, but I believe God will give me peace in the midst of the storm. Enough about me though. How are you feeling? Do you need me to do anything for you?"

"No, it looks like my knight in shining armor has it under control as usual."

"You're right about that. I offered to help, but he turned me down."

"That's Darnell for you."

"I just want to apologize again to the both of you for yesterday. I never thought in a million years Bernard would bring that mess to your home."

"No need to apologize. Nard is who he is. No one can apologize for that, not even him."

"What do you mean by that?" Sharon snaps.

"My bad for speaking ill of your husband. He just isn't one of my favorite people at the moment."

"Breakfast is ready, ladies." Darnell barges in.

"Thank you, baby."

"Wow! This is amazing, Darnell. I really appreciate it. I am grateful to the both of you for having me here in the midst of everything else you have going on."

"Woman, eat your food before it gets cold. You married my boy, you're family now, and this is what we do."

Never in a million years would I have imagined sitting at a table with this woman, being cordial with her. There has to be a special place in heaven for her to even consider me a friend, knowing I'm carrying her ex-husband's child. Let's not forget that Nae and I spanked her real good. Damn, I feel bad about that now that I think about it. I know there's also a special place up there for Darnell as well for putting up with all I've caused. I, on the other hand, probably have an open invitation straight to hell.

"What's the matter, baby girl? Why are you tearing up? Are you thinking about Nariah?" Darnell questions, distracting me from my thoughts.

"Yes, I am. This is going to be harder than I thought," I half lie.

"You have me. You aren't alone in this," Darnell and Sharon sing in unison.

The doorbell chimes. "I got it," Darnell says, springing to his feet.

Just seeing Mona's face brings tears to my eyes as she enters the kitchen behind Darnell. She, Nae, and I were three peas in a pod. This is going to be so difficult for me.

"How are you feeling, pregnant lady?" Mona inquires, kneeling down to hug me.

"Things are better, considering," I blubber.

"If you want, we can do this tomorrow, or I can take care of the arrangements. I put together a few things in place already to alleviate things for you. I hope you don't mind."

"That's a great idea, and we appreciate it, Mona," Darnell interposes.

Chapter Twenty-one

Martinez Is Fed Up

It has been a couple days now, and I haven't heard from Cola. This on-and-off light switch she's regulating our relationship with is becoming a letdown. She claims to have a lot on her mind, but after a year and some change, we should be past this and be able to communicate effectively. This is starting to take me back to when things went downhill with me and Jessica, so I'm going to pull back and give her some space. I can't allow another woman to take my heart to a point of no return, because I won't be responsible for what the man who has a severed heart gives birth to.

I must have thought her up, because she's calling my phone now. "Good afternoon, sexy lady."

"I miss you, *papi*."

"I can't tell."

"I know. I just have so much going on that I shut down."

"Yes, that's what you do best these days."

"You must be upset. You've never spoken to me like this before."

"I'm not upset. Bothered? Yes. Upset? No. I'm just sick of going up and down these stairs with you, Nicole."

"Nicole? When did you start calling me that? What happened to Cola?"

"That's the million-dollar question. You tell me."

"I will fix it, *papi.* I promise I'll make it up to you."

"Sex won't do it this time, sweetness."

"Just give me a couple days to sort things out is all I ask."

"You can take as long as you need, but don't expect me to just lie dormant forever, Nicole. I have feelings too."

Chapter Twenty-two

Sharon Pleads For Forgiveness

I don't know what made me brush my body up against Darnell. What was I thinking? I'm just glad he didn't pick up on it and make an unnecessary scene. Or maybe he did and he's feeling me. I am so attracted to that man's character. Forget his looks. He is the epitome of Boaz in the Bible. *Lord, I know you didn't have me go through all of this to land into Darnell's arms, did you?* You know God has a sense of humor, and I am tickled pink over it, but I'm going to do what the Bible says and be still and know that He is God. All power is in His hands.

What am I thinking? This can't be God. He wouldn't give me a husband while I'm married or while the other man is married. I need to relax. The devil is playing tricks with my mind. What my main focus is and should be is working on my marriage with Bernard. But how do you work something out with someone who is unreasonable, abusive, and unresponsive? He only came by here to get me because I ruined his sexcapade with that lady gigolo. Since Darnell has known my husband longer than I have, I am going to run this by him to see if he can give me some insight, or maybe, when things calm down between the two of them and after the funeral, if he would talk with him for me. I don't know what else to do at this point.

Lord, please forgive me, for my thoughts are far off once again. I need you to purge my mind and cast down every imagination, dear Lord. Right now, I'm here to help Latavia and comfort her, and I need your strength to do so.

"Earth to Sharon."

"I'm sorry, Latavia. I was praying. Are you all right? Do you need anything?"

"You were zoned out over there. Good to know you were praying. I need to get some air along with some clothes. As you can see, I'm beginning to erupt out of everything I own."

"Sure thing. Please allow me to go into the restroom to freshen up, and we can hit the mall. I could use a few things myself."

This has to be a test of my faith from God. She's glowing from the pregnancy, and it is beginning to infuriate me. I don't notice how much she's showing under her clothes until she lifts her shirt. That's supposed to be me pregnant, not her. I was supposed to have Braxton's child, not her. *Lord, please give me the courage to patch things up with Bernard and bless us with a child. I don't want to grow to hate Latavia all over again.*

Chapter Twenty-three

Nicole's Reality

"Granny, it sure smells good up in here."

"Nikki," she echoes coldly.

"What did I do now? I haven't seen you in a week or so, and I'm already getting the cold shoulder."

"Stay in your lane, little girl. You will never be too old to have to pick your teeth up off the floor. Now mind your manners and show some respect."

No matter how old I get, she still calls me little girl. I'm a grown woman. However, I sure do feel like a little girl when I'm around Granny. She has been everything to me. But I don't understand why she's upset with me. I literally just walked through the door.

"What have I done? I just got here."

"Marty, remember him? You'd better stop playing with that man's heart, Nikki. You done messed over on the other one and ended up walking around here snotting and crying all over the place. At this rate, if you keep it up, you're about to be wallowing in your own shit by yourself all over again. A man ain't going to keep putting up with your mess. I don't care how wide you open your legs to him."

Through tears, I sob, "I don't know what's wrong with me, Granny. I'm afraid to trust or allow someone to get close to me. Whether it's a male or female, I make sure to single-handedly destroy the relationship."

"Little girl, you are a beautiful woman. You done had two good men ready to give you the world, and you fell apart before it could happen. I'm surprised Marty gave you the time of day, knowing Darnell had you before he lost all the good sense God gave him and shot your daddy."

"Marty doesn't know about that. They aren't that close when it comes to personal relationships. I was with Darnell. I know how he is. Wait a minute, Granny. What do you mean he shot my daddy? What are you talking about?"

"You must be spending so much time on your back that you can't see what's right in front of you, little girl. You don't watch the news or read a paper?"

"Really, Granny? Why would you say that?"

"The truth can't hurt no more than what you're running around here doing to yourself, little girl."

"Please tell me what you are talking about, Granny. He got in trouble because his wife was messing around on him. He lost it and shot someone was what B—I mean, Bernard—ended up telling me, and yes, I did see it on the news."

"No matter the reason why he got into trouble. The other man the newspeople and paper said he shot was Walter Watkins. You didn't put two and two together? I know you didn't have a relationship with him and his tired ass, God rest the dead, and he didn't exist within the family, but you knew who he was."

"Granny, do you hear what you're saying? That was his wife's father they said he shot, so that means his wife is my sister?"

"This is some *Maury* mess, little girl," she voices, shaking her head in disbelief.

"This is too much for me. I really need to get away. I can't take any more. I came over here to ask you how I could track down Walter, and you just dropped a bomb on me. I never knew my father's last name."

"Stop trying to run and hide from everything, little girl. You need to talk to someone to help you before it's too late."

"I am talking to you right now, Granny."

"And I am not a professional. This is bigger than me, little girl. I want you to really be happy and rid yourself of all that junk that's weighing you down. A man and sex can't fix this for you. Only God and a good shrink."

Chapter Twenty-four

Bernard The Snitch

It is the first of the month and the end of my tour, so it's me and this paperwork before I call it a night, but I can't even think straight reflecting on Sharon's ass. I must be slipping. I'm beginning to miss having her around. She'd better not be over at D's place playing house either.

"What's going on, Martinez," I salute as he trudges over my way.

"Not too much, just trying to maintain."

"Yeah, I can imagine. I heard about you and Nicole."

"Is that right? So what is it you heard?"

"Nah, Carter was just telling me you've been digging her out for a minute now, and he kind of felt bad about it and all, but you know me. I address shit."

"I am a little confused. What are you getting at?"

"Damn, my bad. I thought you knew Carter almost took a leap down the aisle with her, but she played his ass like a cello. Be careful, my man, you know how these broads are."

"Yeah, you're right about that. I'm going to check you later. I've got to go and pick Gabby up in a few."

I am not on no female shit, but he needs to know the truth so Sharon can bring her ass home. I know once shit hits the fan, she's going to pray her ass right on up out of there and carry her juicy ass back home.

Chapter Twenty-five

Darnell's Confrontation

Mona is a godsend. She made all of the arrangements, and the only thing Latavia can do in return is cry. Latavia says that it was as if Mona read her mind and planned everything just the way she'd envisioned it. The service is in two days, and I can't wait to get this over with. I am nervous for my wife. I know this is going to be burdensome for her. I thank God I'm able to be here with her, and I am grateful for Sharon. Despite what I've heard about her and what she's dealing with behind Nard, she has really come through for my wife.

This place is like Grand Central Station, I think, maneuvering toward the door to see who has decided to grace us with their uninvited presence.

"Hey, man, come on in. I've been meaning to shout out to you. Just been caught up trying to handle things on this end."

"I understand, and this is probably the wrong time, but I wanted to have a word with you," Martinez replies.

"No bother at all. What's on your mind?"

"I'm not going to beat around the bush. I'm just going to come out and ask you. Do you know Cola, and did you know her when I showed you the picture of her?"

"I do, and very well, unfortunately."

"Why didn't you say anything?"

"You were already feeling it from your ruined weekend and proposal. I didn't want to add fuel to the already lit fire."

"So were you ever going to tell me, or was I going to have to wait until I ended up bringing her around and be the one sitting there looking like an ass?"

"No, I was going to say something to you eventually. I was just looking for the right time, man."

"I look like a fool right now."

"No, you don't. She does. I know good and goddamn well she knew we were on the job together. How did you find out anyway? Did she tell you?"

"No, I haven't spoken to her yet. Your partner did. You two were engaged also? I really look like a moron now."

"Yes, we were engaged, but that was long ago in the past. There's really no need to go back there, honestly. I just want to know what the hell is up with this dude. Why did he feel obligated to tell you that? Maybe it's me, but he's changed up on me dramatically, and I don't know why or what it is."

"Maybe you're finally seeing the real him who's always been there. He's still the same prick I've always known him to be."

"I don't know what's up, but I will find out. I hate that you had to find out from him. I am sure that didn't go over well."

"You would be correct about that. I felt betrayed because I had to hear it from him, not you."

"I can understand that, but you have to see where I am coming from. You were already upset. Why add to it? You know what I mean?"

"You're right, I do. Well, let me be on my way so I can go have a talk with Cola. None of this is adding up."

"I hear you, man, but on another note, the services are Friday at Greater Bethel. The viewing starts at noon."

"I'll definitely be by to pay my respects. Do you want me to drive you and the missus over?"

"No, we're going over in a limo. You can hop in if you want."

"I'm on call Friday, so I'll just drive over now that I am thinking about it. I'll be in uniform and don't want to make anyone feel uncomfortable, but I will stop by here before the service starts to make sure you're good."

"Thanks, man," I acknowledge before we part ways.

I can't get over Nard. We really need to chop it up. He's on some new shit, and I don't like it one bit. He's supposed to be my boy, but he's crossing me left and right.

Chapter Twenty-six

Latavia Sees The Truth

Being in this mall has me really missing Nae. This was our stress reliever. I can't believe she's really gone, especially since we weren't on speaking terms and didn't get a chance to patch things up. Now I have become joined at the hip with her supposed ex-lover. Don't get me wrong, I have grown quite fond of Sharon. I'm just still in awe of it all.

"Are you all right over there, Latavia?" Sharon investigates, distracting me from my thoughts.

"I'm fine. Just thinking about Nae. We have some history in this mall, so it's making me a little mournful. Maybe it was a bad idea to come out today. The clothes can wait."

"Why don't we go back downstairs to the food court and grab a bite to eat? If you still feel uncomfortable afterward, we can be on our way. How does that sound?"

"You mentioned food, so it's music to our ears," I joke, grabbing my protruding kangaroo pouch.

"Great. After you," Sharon suggests as we approach the escalator.

"Oh, my God," I blurt, trying to catch my balance as I trip stepping onto the escalator. Not able to keep control myself or regain my balance, I tumble all the way down to the bottom.

"Jesus, Latavia, are you all right?" Sharon cries.

"I hope the baby is all right. Can you take my phone, call Darnell, and tell him to meet me at the emergency room?"

"The baby is fine. I don't see any blood. You don't need to keep bothering Darnell about Braxton's baby."

"Excuse me?"

"I'm sorry, Latavia. I didn't mean to say that. It came out the wrong way."

"It's cool. I understand," I fabricate.

Evidently Miss Sharon still feels some kind of way, and the truth is coming out. Why is she at my house and around me if she has a problem with me? Well, we won't have to wonder any longer. Once we get back to the house after I go to the ER to get checked out, I'm going to tell Darnell to ask her to leave. If I'm not mistaken, it felt like she shoved me and played it off like she was try-ing to catch me.

"Are you sure?"

"Yes, I am. Can you hand me my bag so I can call my husband?"

"Ma'am, are you all right? Don't move. I called an ambulance," the mall security guard interrupts.

"I think I will be all right, sir. I'm calling my husband now to meet me over at the hospital," I reply, placing the phone to my ear as it rings.

"What's wrong, baby girl? You miss me already?" Darnell answers into the phone.

"Baby, I fell down the escalator. An ambulance is on its way to take me to the hospital. Can you meet me there?"

"How the hell did you fall? Martinez is pulling out of the yard now. I'll flag him down and have him take me there. Are you sure you're all right?"

"I hope so, babe."

Chapter Twenty-seven

The Other Side Of Sharon

I don't know what has come over me. I saw Latavia stumble, and my mind went to prevent her from falling, but my hand sort of, kind of, nudged her. Evidently, every time she gestures to, displays, or makes mention of her unborn child and extended abdomen, something comes over me. God knows I don't want to hurt her or her unborn love child. I'm just a tad bit jealous because of it all.

Lord, if there were ever a time I needed you, it's now.

This has to be the trial of all time. I am now riding in the back of an ambulance with Latavia. They have her shirt raised, exposing her baby bump. I pray everything is all right. I just can't seem to fight this covetous spirit that's consuming me. The tenth commandment says we should not covet anything that belongs to our neighbor, but what do you do when your neighbor's pilfering habits rob you of your happiness?

Lost in my own mental time capsule, I don't even realize we're already at the hospital, and of course, Latavia's hero beats us here. They sure don't make men like Darnell anymore. God broke the mold when He created that chocolate one there.

"Thank you for being there for my wife, Sharon," Darnell says, recognizing what I did as he approached the ambulance.

"No need. I'm just glad I was there for her, but I'm quite sure she'll be fine. This was more than likely a wasted trip."

"We'll allow the professionals to do their job and come to that conclusion."

"You're absolutely right and I agree."

Lord, please bridle this unruly tongue of mine. It is completely out of control today. Hopefully, we are in and out of here. I need to go home and make amends with my husband. It appears I am projecting my frustrations on Latavia, and that is clearly not of God.

Chapter Twenty-eight

Martinez Reflects

There must be a dark cloud over Officer Carter and his wife. Something is always happening. I was all worked up on the drive over as if it were my wife. The two of them have been through the ringer, especially Carter. That man has sacrificed so much for his wife and his marriage. If I didn't know what love was, he parades the true essence of it by his actions alone. Personally, there's no way I could have done anything remotely close to what he did—either for Jessica when we were married or for Cola now—and lose everything I've worked so hard for. I'm just honored he trusted me with his plan when Officer Peterson is his right hand. That's his boy and all, but I know Carter, and he has to see right through him, which is why his recipe ended up working out perfectly.

He is really a selfless man, and that's not on no homo stuff either. After I shared with him what went down while he was in the coma, he was eager to go find his wife. Once we traced her whereabouts, it was on from there. Just sitting here reflecting on it makes me look up to him even more.

"Martinez, this is all on me. I don't want you to get caught up in my bullshit, so I'm going to catch a taxi

to the hotel and enter through the back entrance. You meet me there in the stairwell just in case something transpires."

"Are you sure? I have no problem escorting you over there, man."

"Cameras are everywhere, and you know that. I don't want you to take the fall for anything that may or may not happen."

"Gotcha. I'll meet you in the stairwell, but if I don't link up with you within ten minutes, I am coming to find you."

When we met up in the stairwell, he struggled walking up the steps, but he was so determined to bring his wife home. I assumed she was his muse and she gave him the strength and energy he needed, because he didn't look too good from where I was standing. However, once we reached the fourth floor, I was instructed to stay put, but it was difficult after sitting there for only about five minutes. As soon as I moved closer to the door to exit the stairwell, I heard a series of gunshots and was unsure where they were coming from. Looking through the glass window in the stairwell door, my eyes landed on the back of Peterson while he was talking to Carter, who was staring in my direction, instructing me with his eyes to stay put.

Immediately after Peterson walked away from Carter and the utility closet, Carter managed to come to the stairwell. With difficulty, he instructed, "Martinez, I did what I had to do. Now leave. No one saw you, and you were never here. You have a daughter to raise. Let me deal with this. I appreciate you and won't forget what you've done for me. Now get out of here, please."

"I can't do that to you, man. You will face time for this."

"*If you do as I say, I won't physically see a jail cell. Now take my word, Martinez, and get the hell out of here.*"

That was the last time I saw or spoke to Carter until his trial. That was the hardest thing in the world to do, but I had to do it for Gabby and for Carter.

Chapter Twenty-nine

Darnell Isn't Feeling Sharon

I'm not quick to jump to conclusions, but Sharon is on some shit. Who gave her the authority to determine whether this is an unnecessary trip? It's better to be safe than sorry. That remark didn't go over well and got under my skin no matter how well she tried to polish it up. In any event, I am just glad my wife is good and the baby is fine. It was pretty amazing hearing the heartbeat and seeing the sonogram of the little one. It's just unfortunate that's not my seed up in there, but I vowed for better or worse.

"Martinez, everything is good. We're just waiting for the discharge papers, so if you need to head out, I most definitely understand. We'll just hop in a cab."

"What's with you and these taxis?" he jokes, I'm assuming in hopes of trying to diffuse the situation.

Chuckling, I reply, "Hey, they can come in handy sometimes."

"We left Latavia's car at the mall. If you want, on our way back, you can swing me by, and I'll pick it up for you," Sharon inserts.

"I just want to get my wife home first. We can get the car later."

"Did you forget about me?" Latavia jokes as the nurse escorts her via a wheelchair closer to us.

"Now you know better than that, beautiful."

"I'm going to bring the car around, Carter. I'll meet you guys out front."

The ride back to the house is a silent one. I am not sure why, but there is an awkward silence. Latavia is staring out the window, and Sharon is staring straight ahead as if she's in a trance or something. I can't put my finger on it, but there's something about that woman that rubs me the wrong way.

Maybe the feeling I had was the surprise of Bernard awaiting our arrival. "We really don't need the drama right now. Sharon, did you invite your husband back over?" I ask.

"No, I didn't, but he and I need to talk, so it's a blessing in disguise the way I see it," Sharon responds.

"Or a curse, if you're observing from where I'm sitting," Latavia interjects.

"I could say the same in Darnell's defense," Sharon snaps back.

"I don't need any defending. Now the both of you kill all of that going back and forth. This has been a stressful time for all of us."

"Pardon me, baby, but I want to know what it is she's trying to say."

"Let's just get out of the car and leave well enough alone, Latavia. You don't need this right now."

"That would be my advice to you, Darnell," Sharon quips.

"And what might that be, Sharon?"

"Leave well enough, or in this case, Latavia alone. I don't understand how you're okay with your wife having another man's child."

"I hope you're okay with this," Latavia blasted before slapping Sharon across the face.

"Latavia, calm your ass down. You're pregnant. Act like a damn lady," I reprimand her.

"A lady, you say? She doesn't know how to be that," Nard scolds her.

"I already told you once about disrespecting my place and my woman, so you'd better go ahead with that."

"What do you mean? She disrespects herself all by herself. I'm just stating the facts."

"Please let's not do this," Martinez and Sharon plead simultaneously.

Before I lose all of my sanity, I take Latavia by the arm and march us into the house.

"Darnell, please ask her to leave and go home with her nasty husband."

"A woman calling names like a four-year-old won't solve anything."

"It won't, but I hate him. You have no idea what he did to me while you weren't here."

"What the fuck do you mean, what he did to you?"

"I was taking a bath. He walked in the bathroom and touched my breast after snatching my towel off me, talking about he'd never had sex with a pregnant woman before."

Chapter Thirty

Martinez In The Middle

If I didn't know better, I would swear this is really the MGM Grand Garden Arena with all the heavyweight bouts trying to take place or that had taken place over here at Carter's place. I thought it was a little strange that Mrs. Carter and Sharon had become bosom buddies with all that has transpired. Looks like my mental telepathy was a sure win the way they went at one another. Now Peterson is going to the door. This can't be good.

"Hey, why don't we give them time to unwind, and we all can come back later?"

"Why don't you mind your business and let me handle this?" Peterson remarks.

"I understand, but everyone is upset right now, and nothing good can come of this. Don't you think?"

"What I think is you should be considering backing up. This has nothing to do with you."

Before I can say another word, the door swings open, and the men I've known to be brothers from another mother who would give their right arm for one another stand toe-to-toe and face-to-face in a very unfriendly manner. If I didn't know better, I'd swear I could see fumes coming from the both of them. That's how thick the tension between them is right now. However, before things can escalate any further, I pin myself between them, saying, "I don't know what this is really about, but you two are officers of the law and, most importantly, friends. This is not how we handle things. There has to be a better way."

"There are only two officers here the way I see it," Peterson mocks.

"Exactly! So that means this civilian has the right to whoop your punk ass. How are you going to disrespect me and my wife, you coward?" Darnell spits.

"Carter, he isn't worth it," I throw in, pushing him back into the house, not realizing Peterson is right on my heels, not backing down.

"I got your punk, D."

"Baby, please let's just go home," Sharon pleads, trying to prevent Peterson from going inside. "What is she doing here, Bernard?" Sharon cries.

"Why in God's name are you at my house, Nicole?" Darnell blasts.

"How do you know her, Darnell?" Sharon asks.

"Why is that your concern, Sharon?"

"She's the reason I left home."

"Sharon, get your ass in the car and wait for me there," Bernard demands.

"No, I'm not going anywhere. It looks like we need to clear the air," Sharon rebuts.

"Cola? What are you doing here?"

"I apologize, *papi.* There's so much I need to tell you, but I need to have a word with Latavia first."

"Oh, shit, D. You've been creeping on the missus?"

"Yo, B, shut the fuck up! Nicole, what is it you feel the need to speak to my wife about?"

"I am sorry. Do I know you? Nicole? Is that what you said your name was?" Latavia inquires.

"Yes, that's my name. Maybe I should come back another time when we can talk privately."

"What? Are you offering your services to them now as well?" Sharon snaps.

"Services, Cola? What's going on?"

"Is that your prostitute name?" Sharon ridicules her.

"Excuse me, but please watch how you talk to her," I defend her.

"Why are you shielding her? She destroyed my marriage."

"I didn't do anything you didn't want me to do. Your marriage was demolished long before you met me, sweetheart. Let's make that clear."

"Cola, what is she talking about?"

Before she can muster up a response, Sharon blurts, "My husband hired her to add spice to our bedroom."

"Damn, B, I see you love eating after me," Darnell mocks.

"Hold up! You slept with them, Cola, and you are a prostitute?"

"I am not a prostitute! Can we discuss this another time, *papi?*"

"William is my name, and from the looks of things, you have one too many *papis*. This is unbelievable, Nicole."

"Please let me explain, *papi.* Don't give up on me."

Chapter Thirty-one

Darnell's Breakdown

This is some shit right here. My boy is on some pristine shit, I see. I didn't sweat it when he was digging Nariah out. She was just something I did at the time, so no sweat was off my back. But Nicole? I was going to marry her, and he invites her to bed with his wife? I guess I don't know this dude like I thought I did after all these years. Now they have Martinez sitting here looking confused and heartbroken. All of this mess is bad timing and something just short of a nightmare, if you ask me.

"Darnell, please ask all of them to leave. I can't deal with this right now," Latavia pleads.

"I am truly sorry for coming by unannounced, Latavia and Darnell, but I would love to sit down and talk with the two of you when you have time."

"Don't fall for it, Latavia. She's already come between me and Bernard—literally," Sharon says.

"That's some shit, B," I say, interrupting Sharon's sermon before it gets started.

"Hell, she threw it at me, D, and I caught it. What man is going to turn down a threesome with no strings attached, especially when his other half is down?"

"When your boy was going to marry the skank, that's when."

"Marry her, Bernard? He was going to marry her, and you brought her to our bed? Our sacred place?"

"Sharon, shut the fuck up, and go and sit your ass in the car like I told you to do before!"

"No, you go to the car! I hate you!" she screams, storming past Martinez, knocking into him so hard they both lose their balance and tumble onto the floor.

"Listen here, everyone!" I shout. "This isn't Grand Central Station or WrestleMania. I want each and every one of you to leave right now. There is nothing else to talk about. Martinez, I will check with you later, and I'm sorry you had to find out about her like this."

"I'm not going anywhere until I finish this," Sharon says, struggling to her feet with her back toward everyone.

"Shut the fuck up, Sharon!" Bernard reprimands her.

"No, you shut up!" Sharon replies, aiming what appears to be Martinez's pistol at him.

"Oh, shit, Carter! She must have grabbed my piece when we fell!" Martinez frantically cries.

"He isn't worth it, Sharon. Please put the gun down before you hurt yourself," Latavia begs.

"Latavia, it would be in your best interest to close your mouth and not say another word, thank you."

"Sharon, what are you going to do with that besides piss me off?" Nard says, agitating the situation.

"You are a poor excuse for a man, and I regret the day I seduced you to try to salvage something that was clearly out of my hands. All of this has done one thing, and that's allowed me to see you for who you are—a no-good piece of horse manure—and myself for a broken woman who has searched for love in all the wrong places. Well, I am done being hurt. It's your turn to hurt!" she cries.

"You need to go pray and calm your ass down and stop pointing that gun at me before you do something you'll regret. What will your God think about that, Sharon?"

"'Until now the kingdom of heaven suffereth violence, and the violent take it by force,'" she recites, releasing three hollow points into Bernard's arm, chest, and face.

"Oh, my God, Sharon, what have you done?" Latavia wails as I stand immobile.

"I thought I told you to be quiet!" she scolds, unable to finish her sentence as Nicole tackles her from behind.

Before anything else can happen, Martinez and I swarm down on her like a pack of flies on shit, disarming her right before Martinez places her in handcuffs. This can't be happening right now. His lifeless body is lying on the floor with blood oozing out of him.

"Darnell, what are you doing? You're not supposed to touch him until help comes. I am calling nine-one-one now. Just give them time to get here please, babe."

Her words fly over my head and smack into the wall and fall on deaf ears.

"Damn, B, it didn't have to end like this. This isn't how we were supposed to go out. I am so sorry we allowed life to fuck us and turn us against one another. How can I go on without my main man? I love you, man, and I'm sorry. Just get up, B! We can work through all of the bullshit, and we'll get you cleaned up with a nice little nurse to wait on you hand and foot. But you have to get up, B!" I cry into my boy's ears, hoping he will catch on to my words and open his eyes, showing me he's good.

"Carter, the medics are here. You have to let him go, man," Martinez pleads.

"He's going to wake up. Give him time. He's just in shock. I got him though. Just be cool. He's going to get up."

"I'm sorry, Carter, but he's gone. You have to let them do their job, man. I'm so sorry," Martinez consoles me, embracing me as if I were his child.

"I can't let go. He needs me, Martinez. He needs me. We have to be strong for him so he can open his eyes."

"You're right, Carter. Let's allow the medics to check him out though. They know what to do better than we do."

Releasing my grip makes room for a flood of emotions to overtake me, causing me to tremble and cry like a newborn. I've seen death before, and I may have caused a couple on the force, but never in a million years would I have imagined this or have been prepared for it. I know he was wrong at times and did most of his thinking with his third eye, but at the end of the day, he didn't deserve to go out like this.

Chapter Thirty-two

Sharon Is Weary

Everything happened so fast I didn't even have time to think. All I heard were the cold words drifting from Bernard's mouth, and then the scripture from the Gospel of Mark devoured me, prompting me to expose Satan for who he is. There's no way he loved me. Love is patient and love is kind. It protects. It does not disrespect, humiliate, and embarrass its wife.

I know I will have to pay severely for my actions, but he left me no other choice. How could he bed the ex-fiancée of the man he calls his brother? And this same harlot is in a relationship with one of his fellow police officers? Latavia must have an angel watching over her, because she was next. If that Nicole person hadn't distracted me and jumped on me, I would have made sure to put her and her bastard child out of their misery. I am fed up with all of these people thinking they can treat me any kind of way. I have to stand up for myself once and for all.

"Mrs. Peterson, you have the right to remain silent. Anything you say can and will be used against you in a court of law. You have the right to an attorney. If you cannot afford an attorney, one will be provided for you. Do you understand the rights I have just read to you?"

Lost in my one-woman conversation, I don't hear anyone call the police or notice when they arrive until I am approached and read my rights. If they said anything prior to that, I didn't hear them. It is all a blur.

"Yes, I understand."

Walking past Bernard's perished soul cover as Darnell grips him for dear life is when reality sets in, and I come to grips with what I've done. It's a little too late for me to cry and be resentful. The best and only thing I can do right now is repent and face the music. I am not an evil woman. I love with every part of me, and I guess this is love gone badly.

"Oh, my goodness, I am a murderer," I sob.

Chapter Thirty-three

Marty Is Falling Apart

I have no idea what in God's name came over Cola tackling down a woman with a loaded gun. This isn't her fight at all. She could have been the one on the floor instead of B.

"I don't do death well," she blurts before vomiting.

"Cola, are you all right?"

"No, I'm not. I can't stay in here and look at him like this. I have to go. I'm sorry," she whines before running out the door.

"Slow down. You can't keep running, Cola. You have to face the woman in the mirror eventually."

"I don't like her. I hate her. She is an evil, hurt, and wounded woman. Why are you even talking to me?"

"Because my love for you won't just go away like that. Yes, I'm hurt to the core from your actions, but the person they discussed is not the woman I'm in love with."

"I'm very good at putting on a front. You don't know me! I don't even know myself!"

"After today and all that's happened, I can't imagine losing you or just walking away from you," I plead as a lone tear seeps from my right eye.

"Please forgive me. Please help me. I need help. I don't want to hurt anymore. I am tired of living a lie. If I hadn't come here, B would be alive."

"Cola, that was going to happen sooner or later, unfortunately. If you allow me, I'll be there with you every step of the way. I can forgive you, and I know it will take time for everything to be right, but I'm willing to take that step," I confess as she cries in my arms.

I hope and pray I'm doing right by forgiving Cola and giving us another chance at this thing called love. This isn't just about me. My Gabby has grown attached to her as well, and she has been like a second mom to her. Holy shit! Just like Jessica, Cola has a problem keeping her walking sticks closed. Is it me? Do I attract this type of woman? How can I have her around my Gabby when she needs a positive woman in her life? Like Granny. How the hell do I work my way around or through this? I'm stuck between a rock and a hard place.

What was I thinking? How can I forgive or forget when she appears to be into women as well? I'm not trying to compete with that. She went from Carter to me and then to Peterson and his family. Now that I am thinking about it, this really is a tough pill to swallow. What am I to do at this point? I'm tired of trying to persuade this woman to love me, because that's exactly what it feels like I've been doing all this time.

Honestly, I really don't know which way to go on this one. There's no way I can bother Carter or even talk to him about it. For one, he has enough on his plate as it is, and let's not forget how close he is to the situation— in more ways than one. I think I need to pay the wisest woman I know a visit. She might be Cola's granny, but she will spit the truth, the whole truth, and nothing but the truth. My job will be to spit or swallow it.

"Papa!" Gabby cheers, jumping into my arms as soon as I walk into Granny's place.

"Hello, princess."

"Hey, Marty, how are you holding up?" Granny quizzes.

"God knows I've seen better days. It's becoming a bit much, Granny."

"You just remember, no matter what, God won't give you any more than you can bear, no matter how hardheaded you are or how tough the situation is, Marty. I'm really sorry to hear about Bernard and what his wife did to him."

"Yes, that was very difficult for all of us there, but hardheaded? What do you mean?"

"Gabby, go back in the front room, and let me and your daddy talk, sweetheart."

"Yes, ma'am," she replies before dashing down the hall without a care in the world.

Just looking at her reminds and confirms the necessity for me to be cautious with any and every decision I make from here on out to protect that innocence of hers.

"Now back to you, Marty. I spoke to my granddaughter. She didn't give me details, but I know you got caught in the middle of her mess, which explains why you're walking around here with your lip dragging. You're hurt and confused, am I right?"

"Yes, ma'am, you're absolutely right. I love Cola. I just don't understand where we went wrong."

"I'll tell you one place you went wrong is when you fell so deeply in love that you lost yourself somewhere on your way down. You young people need to stop falling in love and stand in love. Once you're down, Marty, it's hell getting back up, and this is your second trip. The main person other than yourself you should be concerned about is that angel in the front room."

"I know, Granny, and she is my main objective. I just thought the three of us could be one big, happy family."

"I don't see where in anything you just said that you're putting yourself and Gabby first, hardhead."

"Why do you keep saying that? How am I hardheaded and not thinking of myself and Gabby?"

"A woman can't save you, son. You have to work on you first, Marty. You want love, but you have to love yourself, baby. When was the last time my grandbaby said she loved you?"

"Verbally? Never. But all the time through her actions."

"Marty, do you hear yourself? You already know something isn't right, and you've been ticking in denial."

"No, it isn't like that, Granny."

"There it is right there—denial. Translation: I don't even know I'm lying. You've been lying to yourself, Marty. Now it's time for you to face the truth. As for Nikki, if it's meant to be, it will be. You can't force God's hand, son."

Chapter Thirty-four

Latavia's Soul Cries

Our home has officially been deemed a crime scene, and the medical persons, detectives, coroner, and everyone else have finally left. If Darnell and I have any sense, we will run, not walk, hurrying ourselves up to get the hell out of this haunted home of ours.

"Darnell, there is no way we can stay here. We need a new house or something. This place is cursed. Too many bad things have happened at our threshold," I speak through tears.

Not realizing I'm talking to myself, I turn to face my husband to see my words have evaporated in the air. Darnell is nowhere to be found. He is here physically, but mentally and emotionally he is unavailable, still sitting in the same spot, gazing at the residue of what is left behind from his expired partner and best friend.

I don't know what to do with myself. I want to help him, but I can't. I want to be strong, but I'm weak. How can I console him when I need consoling? My heart aches because, deep down inside, I know this is all my fault. I killed him and Nae. I may not have pulled the trigger or mutilated my sister's body, but my selfish actions assassinated their very beings.

"Darnell, I'm so sorry, baby. Please tell me what I can do to make it right and help you through this. Please, baby, I'm so sorry," I groan, wrapping my arms around him as I make my way down to his level.

The doorbell resonates.

"Who the hell is here now? We can't take any more! Just go away!" I roar.

"I'm sorry, Latavia. I just saw on the news what happened, and I rushed right over. I hope you don't mind I brought my husband with me. He knew Officer Peterson and informed me that Nariah was an inmate at the facility he works at," Mona divulges as soon as she lets herself into the house.

"Now isn't a good time, Mona. We need to be alone."

"I understand, but I won't take no for an answer. I will grab some things for the both of you, and you two can stay in our guest bedroom for however long you need. Please allow us to help you," she pleads through her own waterfall.

Chapter Thirty-five

Darnell Seeks Closure

I must have been anesthetized for a minute and had a loss of consciousness. I don't have a clue where I am or how the hell I got here.

"Latavia, this may sound strange, and I'm not crazy, but where the hell are we?"

"Good morning, my love. We're at Mona's place. She and her husband offered their guest bedroom to us," she replies through a stream of tears.

"We will get through this, baby girl. I promise."

"Do you remember anything that happened yesterday?"

"I don't think I can forget that even if I tried. My heart has a puncture in it that can't be repaired. I do know I have to try to be strong for you and try to move on with the pain that arises with every move I make from here on out."

"I can have Mona help with the arrangements, babe."

"That's cool, but I'll take the lead and work things out with the department since they'll cover the cost."

"Are you sure you're up to it?"

"I owe it to B. I don't have a choice. I'm going to go by his place to see what I can find to try to piece things together."

"Babe, they know who did it. What else are you looking for?"

"I honestly don't know, but I lost him somewhere, and I'm hoping to find out where."

"Don't you think it's too soon for that?"

"I have to do this for me, baby girl."

"Well, I'm coming with you."

"I'll have Martinez transport me, Latavia. You stay here and get some rest."

I have no clue what I'm looking for. All I know is that B switched up on me. He hasn't been himself since the accident. I am the one who had the collision with a head injury, not him. Trying to hold it together right now is eating away at me. I'm not the crying type, but even with all of the man I am, I can't stop myself from shedding tears for my boy no matter how hard I try to hold them back.

Chapter Thirty-six

Latavia Can't Deal

It is unbelievable how Darnell and I lost the closest people next to family we had left around the same time, and we were both at odds with the both of them. We are trying to be strong for one another, but it's difficult. We've spent our evenings holding one another, crying ourselves to sleep. Mona and her husband, Delvin, have been the best hosts we could have asked for. It feels like we are staying in a five-star hotel. They make sure we have fresh linen every day and a meal every time I turn around. I haven't had much of an appetite. Every time I close my eyes or think about food, I see Nard lying on the floor with blood escaping from his form.

Darnell has been spending a lot of time at Nard's place along with Martinez. They are looking for something. What? I have no idea. The police have Sharon in custody, and she pled guilty after pretty much losing her mind. From what Martinez shared, she started banging her head against the wall until she was bleeding, reciting, "By His stripes I am healed." My momma said the Bible is food for the soul, and I agree 100 percent. As for Sharon's case, I think she ate too much, and she is now regurgitating everything she took in.

"Can I get you anything?" Mona asks, snatching me from my one-woman conversation.

"I don't have much of an appetite, but thank you, Mona."

"Latavia, you have to try to eat. You're eating for two now, and you'll need all of your strength for tomorrow."

"Tomorrow?"

"Yes, for Nariah's homegoing service."

"I guess I blocked it out of my mind," I say in grief.

"It's going to be all right. She is in a better place now, Latavia."

"How is it better? She wasn't sick, Mona. I didn't even get a chance to apologize or say goodbye to her. I didn't get a chance to say goodbye to my sister," I bawl.

"Where she is is far better than where she has been, and you will get a chance to apologize to her tomorrow. No goodbye is needed because you will see her when you get to heaven. She's holding a seat for you."

"She won't hear me. I am afraid to see her like that."

"Yes, she will hear you. She's only sleeping until the good Lord wakes her up."

"You sound like my momma, Mona. Thank you. What would I have done without you and Darnell by my side?" I sob.

"I do know that if the shoe were on the other foot, you would do the same for me. This will be hard for the both of us, but we will get through it together."

Chapter Thirty-seven

Martinez Is Torn

I haven't seen or spoken to Nicole, my Cola, in a couple of days now. When I do drop Gabby off at Granny's and she's there, she will stay in the back room or hide in the restroom. Granny said we both need time to heal and to let it be what it is. I have to agree with her because right now I don't think I can look at her the same. Now when I think of her, I end up thinking of Jessica—two different women, different upbringings and nationalities, yet the same, and I managed to fall in love with both of them. I must be the one with the problem. People say when you don't grow up with a mother or a father, you have mommy or daddy issues, depending on the absent parent, but I had both growing up, so what the hell is my problem?

Assisting Carter with packing up and going through Officer Peterson's personals has kept my mind under wraps and off entertaining my torn, conflicted heart. We just got back from retrieving his property, and I think this will be Carter's official breaking point.

I'm just glad I can be here for him and his wife won't have to witness his meltdown, I think as I sit on the sofa beside him. I ask, "Do you want me to go through it?"

"No, I have to do this. I owe it to B. I have no clue what I'm looking for when all I have here is his wallet and his cell phone."

"His phone is probably the best place to start, but how will we get into it without his password?"

"Martinez, when I tell you we had each other's back, I mean just that. We made sure to prepare for this in case something happened to one of us on the job. The peculiar thing is, we weren't on the job when this bullshit happened," he growls, slamming the phone down on the coffee table.

"Look, we don't have to do this now. The service for Nariah is tomorrow. Right now, the best thing you can do is go back to the house and comfort your wife. This is going to be difficult for the both of you. We can do this part another time."

"You're right, but I am going to take his phone and wallet with me. If I find anything, I'll let you know. Thank you for everything, Martinez."

"No thanks needed."

Chapter Thirty-eight

Darnell Searches For Answers

"Babe, why are you up playing with that phone? Whose phone is it anyway?"

"I am sorry to have awakened you. I couldn't sleep. This is B's phone. I'm going through his text messages. I don't know why, but I feel like something is in there."

"Darnell, please look at me. There can't be anything in there to explain why Nard was the way he was. He's always been like that. This is nothing new to you. Now can you please put that phone down and come and lie with your wife? I really need you right now."

"You're right, baby girl. I don't know why I'm tripping. B has always had a way to him, but he just never acted like that toward me before. That's what has me a little fucked up."

"He never had a reason to until now, babe. I'm sorry everything played out the way it did. I wish I could rewind the hands of time all the way back and not have run out the way I did. Had I not, Nae and Nard would still be here. It's all my fault," she cries into my chest.

"It's not your fault. Now stop blaming yourself, Latavia."

I know it isn't her fault, but she has a point. If she had stayed and talked to us like an adult, we wouldn't be in a couple of the predicaments we are in now. But I don't know that to be true, because the old lady taught me that everything happens for a reason. I look at it like this: if it hadn't been them, it could possibly have been one of us. I just wish it didn't have to be anybody. Now we have to prepare ourselves for tomorrow and for my boy the following week. *Lord, I am going to need a boatload of strength for this, because a brother is feeling a little frail right about now.*

Chapter Thirty-nine

Nicole Faces Her Reality

Although my *papi* said he would be here for me every step of the way, I can't allow it. All my life, I've allowed my meat-packing district—formerly known as my va-jayjay—to reign and rule over my life. All my decisions have been based on emotions and sex, and I can't go on the rest of my life like this. I've been hurting long enough and have been covering it up with sex, along with my evil ways. Granny laid into me real good when I confided in her about how things played out between me and her Marty. She loves that man like her natural-born son, and I can't take that away from her or Gabby. I love that little girl, but I'm no good for her right now.

I started seeing a shrink yesterday, and talking to him felt like I was piercing myself in the same open wound over and over again. I wish I could go away some place inpatient to get the help I so desperately need. I'm afraid of myself at this point. Granny said that if I can get out of my lease, I can stay with her, but when Marty and Gabby are around, I have to find something to do quietly in my room. I don't like the sound of that at all, but I need the space to get myself together, and I need Granny to get through it. At this point, it will be work and home for me like I'm on punishment, but I know it's for the best.

Dear Diary:

I know I haven't spoken with you in such a long time. I really wish you were a real friend, not me talking to myself about myself. Had you been a real and true friend, you could have told me about my devilish, whorish ways. I don't blame you. I did this to myself. I just wanted to write to you one last time to let you know I'm moving on with my life to try to better myself.

I am going to give my doctor this notebook and the others so he can see the real me, just in case I try to hide something. I didn't realize how messed up I was until I saw someone's life taken right before me. I started out on this last crazy journey of mine on a mission to take back a man who never belonged to me in the first place, only to end up alone and by myself as usual.

What I have learned in the last twenty-four hours is that sex is a physical act that lasts for an hour or so but has the capability to damage your very being for a lifetime. Be careful how you use that deadly weapon between your legs. It can and will kill you in more ways than one.

I'm going on and on as usual, but I find solace in writing down my thoughts. So thank you for listening, my dear friend and diary.

Love Always,
The Woman in Broken Pieces

Chapter Forty

Sharon Loses Herself

"For the Lord heareth the poor and despiseth not me as a prisoner. You can't chain a woman who has been set free. He who the Son sets free is free indeed. I am a free woman. Loose me, demons!" I wail in agony.

I don't know what came over me when I was banging my head against the wall. The next thing I know, blood is gushing everywhere, blurring my vision, and all I can see are Braxton and Bernard lying at my feet, riddled with bullet holes. I don't know why they chained me to this bed when I only bumped my head on the wall a little too hard. They panicked, injecting me with drugs to put me to sleep. I told them I could fall asleep on my own, but these new-age police doctors think they know everything. They won't even allow me to attend either of my husbands' memorials. Every married couple has spats. Ours just got a little out of control.

"God forgave me for my mistakes, so you have to let me out of here!" I rant into the air because no one listens to me when I talk to them anyway.

Oh, my goodness, I was supposed to help Latavia with the funeral arrangements for Nariah. I hope I didn't miss the services.

"Hello? Someone please listen to me. I can't stay here! I need three bereavement passes. I have to bury both of my husbands and help a friend. Didn't you see my husbands on the floor? I need closure. I have to see my husbands off. You can't keep me in here like this. I have rights! Loose me, demons! Loose me . . ." I mumble as the police doctor administers another dose of what appears to be my sleeping medicine.

Chapter Forty-one

Darnell Comforts Latavia

"Baby girl, I'm right here with you. I won't leave your side. You can do this."

"Darnell, I can't walk up there and look at her in that box. I'm not going in there."

"Latavia, you won't be able to rest if you don't go in there and pay your respects to your sister. Now please take my hand, and let's go up there to see your sister off the right way."

"I can't," she cries with every step she takes toward the front of the church.

Hell, I'm feeling a little woozy, and my legs feel like they're about to give out. Shit! This isn't supposed to happen now. I have no real attachments to this woman other than through my wife. I guess I am feeling my wife's pain.

"Hey, buddy, let me usher you two up front," Martinez rescues us.

"Thank you," I whisper.

"Darnell, can I have a moment alone with her please?" Latavia questions as we reached the wooden overcoat that holds her sister-friend.

"Are you sure?"

"Yes, I am babe," she whimpers.

"I'll be standing right here behind you. I won't leave your side."

It's evident at this moment that I am nowhere near as cut out for this as I thought I was. Standing here watching my wife kiss and lay her face against Nariah's corpse, while silently crying and whispering in her ear, is eating away at me like an old bedsore. I don't think I've cried this much since the old lady went home to be with the Lord. As I look around, I can see the line has grown, along with Mona flying down the aisle with Delvin on her heels. He might as well stand over here with me and allow the women to have their moment. This is a very disheartening time. The three of them have been through so much with building Elite. I know the bond they had together, along with the soul tie Nariah and my wife had.

"Oh, my God. I am sorry, Nariah," a male voice echoes in pain.

When I turn to my right to see where the voice is coming from, Delvin, Mona's husband, is on his knees, whimpering for Nariah. Now I'm no genius, but this can't be right. He didn't say one word to us about Nariah while we were at his house, so what's really going on here? Hold the hell up! When I went through B's phone, there were text messages to and from a DM, but I didn't get a chance to read them because my wife woke up. DM probably stands for Delvin goddamn Michaels. Holy shit!

The service and repast turned out beautiful, just the way I envisioned them, and Nae wouldn't have had it any other way. Mona did right by her with the arrangements, and we are forever indebted to her. I just don't want to be on the other side of this bedroom door with her and Delvin. When he broke down at Nae's homegoing service, I thought Mona was going to body-slam him. If looks could kill . . . Well, you know the ending. I'd rather not speak on it or play with death right now, considering.

"Excuse me, Darnell and Latavia, we need to talk," Mona summons us from the other side of the door.

"Please come in," I invite her.

"First, I would like to say that I'm sorry for all of this. I had no idea, and I am completely mortified."

"Mona, you did nothing wrong," Latavia consoles her, wrapping her arms around her.

"I know I didn't, but the man I vowed to spend the rest of my life with did."

"What are you saying, Mona? You're scaring me," Latavia panics.

"I apologize, Latavia. I had no idea, but my husband has been, or was, having an affair on me."

The silence that brushes through that room like a mighty, rushing wind would make an innocent person paranoid.

"I was wrong, Mona. I am so sorry. We needed the cash, so I did what I needed to do as a man to prevent us from losing our home we've worked so hard for."

"That's what you call being a man, Delvin? A man wouldn't have spent all of our savings and everything else gambling. A real man would not have had an affair with my deceased boss. You knew who she was when she got to your facility. How could you do this to me? To us, Delvin?" she cries uncontrollably.

What the hell did I just hear? This is unbelievable. We have been here for the past few days, and this man never said one word about even knowing Nae. He tagged along and watched Mona make the arrangements, when all along, he had been sleeping with her.

"Delvin, can I speak to you in the other room please?"

"Please do, Darnell. Maybe he'll learn the meaning of what it is to be a real man," Mona scolds him.

"Sure. We can go into the den and talk. It's this way," he directs me, pointing to the left.

"So you knew Nariah?"

"Yes, I did. Officer Peterson approached me with a proposition I couldn't turn down. I had nothing to do with her death. I swear to you I didn't. I had nothing at all to do with it. You have to believe me," he begs.

"All right. Please try to calm down, and tell me everything that happened."

"Like I said, Bernard approached me. After learning where Nariah was, he asked me to find out everything I could. He thought it was strange she didn't hire the best attorney money could buy. He said she was a freak, and I could have my cake and eat it, too—literally. When I saw her face-to-face and up close and personal, I had to try her. I'm sure you know how that is, my brother."

"No, I don't, but continue please."

"Long story short, we went at it the entire time she was there prior to her passing. I was beginning to really feel her. I ain't never had a woman do me like her. Just seeing her up there earlier messed me up real bad. I don't know what came over me. I didn't realize what I was doing until I felt Mona's eyes piercing through me."

"That was a little mind-boggling and pretty much caught everyone off guard."

"Yes, it did, including me. But anyway, she ended up confiding in me and said she didn't shoot or kill anyone."

"Now we both know that half the people in jail have more excuses than a little bit and claim they're innocent."

"When she told me that, I said the same exact thing to her, but she said she had it all on tape. She and her old man were going to make a little sex tape, but she never got a chance to turn it off, and she was able to record everything that transpired."

"On tape? Is that right? Well, if she had everything on tape, why did she sit in that cell all that time and not come forward with it before she got there?"

"Because Peterson covered everything up and pinned it on her, and she took the rap for it. He was an officer of the law, so she felt she couldn't trust anyone because we were all in cahoots. She was a smart broad. She was right about it, and I feel like shit now because of it."

"He covered what up? Did she say he shot Walter?"

"No, she didn't go into details about all of it when she spoke to me."

"So she was lying then?"

"No, she was telling the truth and told me where I could find the camcorder. I gave that information to Peterson."

"For all you know that recorder could have been blank since neither of them are here to vouch for it."

"I saw it for myself, and I made a copy of it prior to informing Peterson about it just in case he tried to pin some shit on me."

"Do you still have the tape?"

"No, I destroyed it when Peterson was . . . you know?"

"Just tell me this—if Nariah didn't shoot that man, what was B trying to cover up? I know for a fact I didn't do it. So who did you see on the tape?"

"Your wife, sir."

"My wife?"

"Yes, when that man walked out of the restroom, your wife saw red and let him have it."

"This isn't a joking matter. My wife could end up doing some serious time for this shit."

"The way I see it, the damage is already done. Unfortunately, Nariah took the rap for her because I'm not saying anything. I could lose my job for getting involved with this mess and thinking with my third leg."

"This is the craziest shit I've ever heard. You're certain you saw my wife on that tape?"

"Yes. I knew who she was from the pictures Mona has of the three of them."

Damn! Latavia ain't crazy. She knows what she did. How could she allow Nariah to sit in prison, knowing good and well she's innocent? Why didn't she tell me? I know none of us wants to sit in a cell—hence why I pled a little crazy, saying Martinez drove me when he didn't—but I would never allow anyone to take the rap for me no matter how mad at B I was.

What else is this woman hiding from me? I guess I didn't know her or B. Neither of them is the person I thought they were.

The day we laid my boy B to rest, pieces of my life, including my happiness, were buried with him. After approximately two months, I haven't been able to sleep. Latavia and I barely talk, and it feels as if I'm married to a pregnant stranger. If the conversation isn't about a doctor's appointment or something pertaining to the baby, mum's the word. I know I was down-and-out after my boy's services and needed time to adjust to everything around me—such as finally being released from the hospital, losing my boy, and the sudden realization that my wife is now happily married to herself while carrying her high school sweetheart's child.

I have never been a jealous man. I have no reason to be. However, when you become one with a person, you feel them even when they don't speak. It is what I like to call a soul connection, and there is definitely something going on with Latavia. And I don't think it's just the pregnancy. Maybe this baby is driving a wedge into the love she has—or had—for me, or there's a strong possibility she never loved me the way I love her. I don't know what it is at this point, and with everything that has transpired with staying with Delvin and Mona, and losing B and Nariah, we're probably so deep in the residue of all of this loss that we can't find ourselves or our happy place.

If the PD hadn't provided immediate grief counseling like they did, I think I would have seriously snapped by now. I've been to dozens of funerals for some of my fellow fallen officers and dealt with it the best I could, but this one hit me like a ton of bricks because it was so close to home. The silence throughout the funeral service among the officers in attendance was so loud you could hear each of our thoughts, thinking this could have been one of us lying here, but in Nard's case, we were also thinking, *how did he let this happen or allow things to go this far?* However, besides the silence, the bagpipe tribute was probably the saddest, most emotional moment in the world. It brought me to my knees, and I cried like a bitch. Nard was a son of a gun at all times, but he was my boy and my brother from another mother. I'm sure no matter what it was he had going on, we would have been able to work through it. Well . . . maybe not, now that I'm thinking about it. He and Latavia were really on some whole other level with their lies and secrets, and they played me like a fiddle.

I have yet to mention to her what Delvin disclosed to me about the tape, because I know if she isn't truthful with me, I'm going to really lose my cool in a not-so-pleasant way. Speaking of Delvin, he and Mona have been the greatest hosts to us, even while working through their own marriage turmoil. We're still staying at their place until we sell our home and find another. I believe staying here has made things a little easier for all of us to avoid our true feelings and problems. Latavia and Mona spend countless hours together between baby talk and Elite. Delvin, on the other hand, is either working or in the den watching television. Two couples under the same roof, and both of our marriages are holding on by a thread.

Chapter Forty-two

Latavia's Disloyalty

I love Darnell with everything in me. However, I don't feel for him like I used to. There was a point in time when the thought of him would cause me to blush or smile or look forward to spending every available moment with him. It was all I craved. That subsided somewhere along the way, because I can't get away from him fast enough these days. Mona said sometimes pregnancy does that to a woman and not to put too much thought into it. Maybe that's what it is. I'm so unsure and confused at this point. Mona, on the other hand, refuses to sleep with her husband, yet she is cordial and treats him as if nothing has happened. His permanent residence just happens to be the den at the present time. It's sad and funny at the same time because of the way Mona acknowledges their current sleeping arrangement.

My hormones are on overdrive from this pregnancy, and I have been having bipolar mood swings that I conveniently take out on my poor husband. I don't do it intentionally. It just comes out. I know I'd better get a handle on it before he does the unthinkable and switches up on me and I end up all alone. Speaking of disorders, my sex drive is now at an all-time high, but the unfortunate thing about it is I can no longer get the satisfaction I long for from Darnell. Oral sex used to be my preference, more so than penetration, but I am just sick of it and don't desire it or him these days. Penetration is all I can think of, but I'm afraid to use my Rabbit on a regular basis because my baby might be born with a trembling disorder if I keep using that thing.

Honestly, I don't know what happened. I've just lost that spark I once had for my husband. I have been trying to find it. However, my recent events put a black eye on everything. I don't know how it got to this point, and I feel awful. I've played the night before Nard's funeral over and over in my head, and I still don't know how it happened. I am far from a homewrecker or an unfaithful woman. When I became intimate with BK, I was under the assumption that Darnell and Nae were having an affair, and the first time I was actually with him was primarily to prove a point. So technically it doesn't count in my book.

In any event, that Thursday before the funeral service, I wasn't feeling well, and Darnell had advised me to stay in and rest up in order to be prepared for the funeral. Mona was at Elite Too preparing for an event, and Delvin and I were the only ones at the house. Anyway, I decided to use the shower in Mona's master bath because she has a Jacuzzi tub in there and said I could use it any time. I had no idea Delvin was in there pleasuring himself and that the sight of it would turn the both of us on—or that we would end up making beautiful, long-overdue music inside the Jacuzzi. He didn't care that I was pregnant by another man. He just wanted to please me, and I made sure to please him back.

Horrible as it was and sounds, it felt so good—so good that I now believe that's where I lost the desire and lust I used to have for Darnell. Delvin and I vowed to never cross that line again and to forget it ever happened. However, every time we're alone, we find ourselves giving in to temptation. This has been going on for a little over a month now . . . actually two months if I'm not mistaken.

Chapter Forty-three

Nicole Is Tired Of Hurting

"Granny, I think something's going on with your Marty."

"Why is it your concern, little girl? You done messed over that man enough. I'd better not catch you anywhere near him. Do you hear me?"

"I'm just saying. I hear how slurred his speech is when he comes to pick up Gabby, plus I see him through the window. He doesn't look like himself. Something is off."

"Hush, child. You don't even know that man the way you should know him."

"If you say so."

I love that old lady to death. She's just so stuck in her ways. Especially still referring to me as a little girl. I'm a grown-ass 31-year-old woman. It used to drive me crazy, but my therapist helped me realize I have been fighting against Granny's love because she is the closest thing to my mother I have left. Basically, I blame Granny for my mother not being the comforting, nurturing, caring, and loving parent she was supposed to be. Instead, she'd poured every ounce of her love and affection into a man—a man who couldn't give two shits about me, or her for that matter. Why in God's name hadn't she seen what she was doing to me? She was a selfish human being, and Granny had given birth to her. How could Granny help me when she'd raised a weak, selfish woman like my mother? Now history is repeating itself, because I am nothing short of a mess.

"Why?"

"Nikki, are you all right? What's going on in that head of yours?"

"How could you have raised someone who turned out like my mother? What kind of person were you to raise someone as selfish as her?"

"First, what you are not going to do is blame everyone for the decisions you made, little girl. A foundation is and was all I was responsible for. It was laid for you as well as your mother. God left us the Bible full of rules, instructions, remedies, and solutions, but it is up to us to choose who we're going to serve. Now you have to make up your mind what you're going to do, because blaming your momma—God rest the dead—and me will get your teeth knocked out. What you need to do is keep talking to that lady because you're going to need her more than you think."

"What's that supposed to mean?"

"It means that each hurdle, revelation, and detail of your life you uncover will bring on a different kind of pain, and my love for you won't fix it. However, talking to your doctor and developing an unbreakable connection with God will make you a whole new person and heal those broken places, baby girl."

Through a thunderstorm of tears, I voiced, "Thank you, Granny. I am so sorry for blaming you."

I don't want to hurt any longer. I need to be a better person in order to progress in my life. This mess has affected everything around me. It is so bad I've had to take a leave of absence from work under my psychiatrist's direction. I haven't shared that information with Granny just yet. I'm a little embarrassed that I'm a head case. My doctor said she couldn't understand how I've maintained this long. Then she explained how I've managed to use my relationships and sex as a drug to numb or avoid the pain.

Look at the time. I need to head on over to Dr. Bergman's office for my appointment. I can't afford to be late. She charges $25 for every fifteen minutes you're late to an appointment—cash only!

Just my luck! As soon as I get to the door, look who's coming out of the building—Darnell.

Chapter Forty-four

Ramona's Heartache

Never in a million years would I have imagined that my husband, the only love I've known or bedded, would have betrayed me in such a way. I have been trying to circle back to see where I went wrong because there had to be something I wasn't doing to make him forsake me and our marriage bed. To stick the knife in deeper, he slept with my boss of all people, a woman he knew I admired and was very fond of. Nariah had a way about her, but what I respected the most was how real and upfront she was about hers. You didn't have to wonder anything about her because she made it known what she was or wasn't doing. If she wanted something, she would do whatever she needed to do to get it—no matter who he belonged to.

Which was why, for me, work was work and my marriage was my marriage. I never brought Delvin around. They had no idea what he looked like. Well, Latavia did. I just kept him far away from Nariah. She used to taunt me, saying, "He must be drop-dead ugly, because you keep him hidden like expensive jewelry or money."

Evidently, I wasted my time playing hide-and-seek, because he didn't give a second thought to who she was, or to our union for that matter. He just had to have a piece of her. I hope he's happy, because it will be a cold day in hell before I allow him to touch me again. More than likely, this won't work in my favor and could possibly sever things between us permanently. I feel so inadequate, unattractive, and humiliated, as if I am unable to satisfy him. Seriously, what other reason did he have to step out on me?

Being a preacher's kid, I was taught to save myself for marriage, so the only man I have ever been with is Delvin. My dad would minister and teach us how important it was to save ourselves for marriage. He said a real man would love, respect, honor, and be 100 percent faithful to his bride that much more because she'd saved herself for him and their special day. Dad said any man who was the one and only to his bride would feel like a king and on top of the world. He would have no reason whatsoever to step out on his wife. I believed his words were true because that had to be the only reason he'd had to step out on my mom the way he had. It had to have been his lack of respect for her, because she hadn't been a virgin when they got married.

Mom lost her virginity and got pregnant on her first experience with sex at the age of 14. During our many talks about the birds and the bees, she would stress the importance of me waiting until I was married to give myself away because she didn't want me to end up like her, which confirmed to me she knew what my dad was doing and she blamed herself. I didn't want to grow up and walk in my mother's footsteps—in constant pain, regretting my life or the decisions I'd made like she did—so I'd made it my business to save myself for my husband.

You would never know my dad was an elder of the church, because I did whatever I wanted to do. I just had a hard time agreeing with all of those rules and Commandments, so I rebelled like hell. As I matured, it all appeared to be a bunch of rules my dad enforced on the congregation as his way of having control over everything and everyone. I think my main problem was that I knew my parents outside of church. Don't get me wrong, I love the both of them to death, and they've taught me a lot and made me the woman I am today. I just knew the real them outside of their church attire and lingo.

Thinking back still troubles me some because I had no clue of the control and emotional abuse I was under or the impact it would have on my life. I was around 15 years of age when things began to unfold, and I would question things as I began to see the truth for what it was. For instance, the women in the church were extremely rude and disrespectful to my mom but would shower me with gifts and love on Dad like he was God Himself.

The first eye-opener for me was on a Sunday afternoon. We'd had evening service as we did every Sunday, which meant dinner downstairs in the kitchen. Mom had to leave service a little early on this particular Sunday to go visit my brother in prison as she did the fourth Sunday of every month. Anyway, I didn't want the church food, as I never did. However, I'd neglected to get spending money from her before she left. I made sure to do something nice to help Dad out before going into his office to ask him for money. Everything was a job for Dad. "You have to give in order to receive," he would chasten me. He took that scripture to heart with everything.

After cleaning up the church and collecting all of the fans and church programs, I packed everything up to bring them to Dad's office where they were stored. Most importantly, I did it to show him my contribution to the sanctuary. Knocking on his office door before entering, I made my presence known by saying, "Pastor, it's your daughter. I cleaned the sanctuary for you and need to put the fans and programs away."

"Give me a min—" he voiced a little too late, because I was already in his office before he could finish his sentence.

Walking in, I hadn't realized or noticed my dad was in the middle of counseling someone or praying for her until I heard him petition God, saying, "Lord, we ask you to forgive, heal, deliver, and set free," as he sat on top of his desk with his back facing me while the person he was praying for was in front of him on the floor.

"Amen," I chimed in, touching and agreeing with my dad.

With his back still facing me, he voiced, "I need you to give me a minute, Mona. Allow me to finish things up here, and as soon as I'm done counseling, I'm all yours."

"No problem, Dad . . . I mean, Pastor."

Out of respect, I refer to my dad as Pastor just like the congregation does because he's my pastor at church and my dad at home. However, as I was leaving the office, something made me look over my shoulder as I turned the doorknob. I could see my dad frantically trying to zip his pants and his "sister," who had just moved back to town, wiping her mouth as she struggled to pick herself up off the floor at the same time.

Chapter Forty-five

Latavia Is Behind Closed Doors

"Delvin, we have to stop doing this. Mona's my friend, and I have been horrible to Darnell when he has been nothing but good to me."

"How are you going to say we have to stop while my dick is practically in your mouth?"

"I guess it's the wrong time to talk about this, but this is the last time!"

"Please just keep doing that thing I like and stop talking, Nariah."

"Okay, that's it. Now I am done! Why do you keep calling me Nae?"

"Shit, my bad, Latavia. You just remind me of her so much. I think that's why and how all of this got started in the first place."

"So you're screwing me because I remind you of my deceased best friend?"

"Woman, you don't even know the meaning of 'friend'!"

"Excuse me?"

"A friend is someone who will be there for you through thick and thin. Support you in everything and put you before herself. She is truthful and honest and allows you to stay in her home for free."

"Hold up. We pay Mona every month for staying here. You need to check with your wife and not come at me with that bull. And how are you going to talk about being honest and trustworthy?"

"My wife knows I was out there and messed up."

"'Was' and 'is' are two different words with two different meanings."

"Either way, I know I fucked up. I have to deal with that, and I've accepted my shit. You're the one who hasn't owned up to anything."

"Regardless of all you've said, that doesn't justify you calling me Nae."

"Look, you and I both know this was something that just happened. I was really feeling Nariah. Believe it or not, both of you give head like professionals. I have never had a woman suck me off like you two."

"You're sick."

"The pregnant woman who happens to be sleeping with the man who had an affair with her best friend and who is the husband of her good friend and employee calls me sick?"

"Fuck you, Delvin!"

"That's what you're supposed to be doing, but you keep spitting things out of your mouth instead of swallowing."

"I hate you!"

"Latavia? Who are you in there talking to?" Darnell quizzes from outside the bathroom door.

"No one, Darnell. I'm all right."

"Open this door or I am going to knock it down, Latavia."

"The hell you are! This is my shit! You won't be knocking a damn thing down!"

Darnell hits the door open so hard it flies open and knocks me into the sink.

"What the fuck is going on in here?"

"He tried to rape me, Darnell!"

"Before or after you were sucking my dick, Latavia?"

No other words are exchanged at this point. I think Darnell sees red. He grabs Delvin and starts choking the life out of him. I try to calm him down, but I'm not strong enough for the two of them.

"Please stop, Darnell! You're going to kill him!"

"Fuck him!"

Delvin squirms and kicks himself loose, and they begin to pound on one another. Before I can get out of the way, a powerful blow to my midsection thrusts me into the wall, causing me to hit my head on the sink. When I look down, I can see blood pouring out of me, and that's the last thing I recall happening before everything goes black.

Chapter Forty-six

Martinez Can't Cope

Ever since the shooting, I have been trying to keep a level head and keep busy to try to avoid my own thoughts. I've tried to come up with different scenarios or things I could have done to prevent Peterson's wife from getting a hold of my piece. The truth of the matter is, no matter what I come up with, she got hold of it, and now Peterson is gone. The department decided to put me on modified duty to allow me time to get myself together. It isn't working. My focus is gone, and my mind is everywhere except on the job. I took it upon myself to put in a request to take a short leave, which no one outside the department knows about. I make sure to get Gabby to Granny's place on time and pick her up at the usual pickup time so I don't blow my cover. I know this charade might be a little difficult and a bit much. I need the time and distance from everything and everyone because I am no good to my baby girl in my current condition.

Honestly, I don't know how it even got to this point. The only thing I remember is the aftermath of a prescription-drug bust a week or two prior to the funeral service that literally changed my life. If I could redo that day all over again, I would have done things differently. My actions have caused me to develop a nasty habit that I'm trying to eliminate, but it's the only way I've been able to cope and sleep at night.

I can recall that day as if it were yesterday, and if I'm not mistaken, that day started off like any other day on the job—or so I'd thought. As soon as I got to the 7th Precinct, the FBI was there, laying out details for a drug raid at a local storefront pharmacy. Apparently, the patients weren't patients, and the doctors wrote and filled prescriptions at the pharmacy—for cash only, of course. In layman's terms, the doctors were selling, prescribing, and filling hydrocodone prescriptions. Without question, the Feds ran the show. We were just the "muscle." To this day, I still can't believe they allowed me to take part in the bust after Peterson's wife used my piece to take him out.

My mind has been all over the place, and more so since that day. Between the shooting and Cola, I haven't been able to get it together. I do my best to remain focused for Gabby. She is my driving force. I just wish that force had shielded me from helping myself to the bag of a thousand pills I confiscated during the bust and stuffed down my pants. I have a low tolerance for drugs and can't stand anyone who abuses them. I have no idea how the thought even crossed my mind or, more importantly, what persuaded me to take them and become dependent on them. Drug and alcohol abuse are a coward's way out to me, so I am not particularly a fan of the man I look at in my mirror every day.

Chapter Forty-seven

Delvin's Drought

Things with Mona and me have been bad but good, considering. She cooks, cleans, caters, and speaks to me as if nothing has happened. The one and only thing—the main thing—missing out of the equation is the strip tease, the horizontal polka. In other words, no hot sex on the platter. No body rocking, knocking the boots. Absolutely nothing at all in that department. I guess you can say I got off a little easy. But her lack of intimacy drove me straight to Latavia. No, she didn't tell me to stray and get caught up. However, after three months of nothing, there's only so much temptation a man can resist. It was so bad that, even when she was on her red-light special—the time when almost every woman is her horniest—she didn't budge. Mona said she thought she was going through a bad case of early menopause because her desire for sex had subsided, and she couldn't explain how or why it was happening.

When she and I first met, we couldn't get enough of each other, but when we got married, it was at a whole other level. Our lovemaking was so good I could have been a spokesperson or an advocate for the married life, because it was wetter, tighter, and deeper. No bullshit!

You would think she'd had a kitty change or an implant or something. Let's not forget the text messages I would receive during the day just because. They weren't your average texts either. She would send the ones that would send a signal, an APB, or a notice to my manhood, alerting him, "We've got action!" I couldn't wait to get home! How can I forget the surprise visits to the job? The last visit was so long ago, but I remember it like it was yesterday—or this morning. Damn, I miss those days!

Mona: Delvin, I mean daddy, I know you had me squirming and screaming this morning, but my kitty won't stop purring. She's still hungry. Can you feed her?

Me: Damn, baby girl! As soon as I get in, I will take care of her, I promise.

Mona: I don't think she can wait that long. She's foaming at the lips right now, and I can't control it.

Me: Shit, Mona! You've got me rock hard, woman.

Mona: Take lunch, and meet me in the parking lot.

Damn, just thinking about that shit has me at full attention. I guess I'd better head to the master bath and do what I've been doing for the last few months to take care of this load. "Shit, baby," I moan as thoughts of my wife and flashbacks of Nariah invade my mind, forcing me to stroke myself faster.

"Oh, my God, Delvin! I'm sorry. I didn't know anyone was in here," Latavia apologizes after barging into the restroom.

Damn, this is awkward and embarrassing.

There's nothing I can say or do to make this better. I am almost there, so I do what any man would do in hopes she will find her way back out the door so I can pick up where I left off to try to bring my erection back.

"You're just going to do that in front of me, Delvin?"

"Either you're going to help me out, or you're going to get out. The choice is yours."

"I don't know what to do."

"Whatever your body is telling you to do," I retort, facing her as I stroke my fully loaded pistol.

Instead of leaving, she positions herself to make it easy for her to ease into a sitting position on the toilet and pull me closer to her as she introduces my hole punch to her mouth.

"Fuck! Oh, my God, Nariah . . . inmate . . . I mean, Latavia."

Chapter Forty-eight

Darnell's Whammy

As songstress Aaliyah's voice sang the lyrics to "The One I Gave My Heart To" through the speakers, tears threatened my eyes.

How could the one I was so true to
Just tell me lies?
How could the one I gave my heart to
Break this heart of mine, tell me?

I think I'm getting a little soft in my old age. I guess with everything that's going on around me and the words to this song, damn, I must be in my feelings a little bit, as Latavia would say. Hell, the way I see it, if I didn't have feelings, I wouldn't be able to love her the way I do. That doesn't make me soft at all. I just want to know why the hell Dr. Bergman feels that song is an appropriate tune to blast in the lobby. Is she trying to use musical therapy to break us down before she sees her patients? I can't take too much more of this. I think I need to go to the house and have a heart-to-heart with my wife.

"Maureen, I have an emergency. I need to reschedule."

"Sure thing, Mr. Carter."

"I'll call to set up a new appointment. Thank you."

I have to hurry up and get the hell out of here. Dr. Bergman must have that song on repeat. It has been playing for like twelve minutes. What the hell is wrong with her?

"Darnell?" a voice rang out, distracting me from my one-man conversation.

Oh, shit, not this woman! "What the hell do you want, Nicole? Why are you following me? How did you even know I was here?"

"I hate to be the bearer of bad news, but you aren't the only one who requires a head doctor, love."

"Great! Just my luck. Every time I turn around, your ass is there all of a sudden. Why don't you go back to wherever it is you were? You've caused enough problems."

"I acknowledge the part I've played in some of your troubles, but you will not blame it all on me. I wasn't in your marriage picture long enough to cause anything."

"Whatever, Nicole."

"Wait a minute, Darnell. I need to talk to you about something. I was hoping I could sit down and speak with you and Latavia."

"What in God's name do you need to speak to my wife about? She doesn't know you and doesn't need or want to. So what's up?"

"It would be better if I talked to her myself."

"I'm out and this conversation is done," I throw over my shoulder as I proceed to walk away.

"Latavia is my sister, Darnell," she rebuts a little over a whisper but loud enough to stop me dead in my tracks.

What the fuck? "Are you going crazy? How can Latavia be your sister? Remember we dated for years, and you met your father one time and couldn't recognize him in a crowd. So how is it that now, all of a sudden, you know who he is, and he just so happens to be my wife's father?"

"I know it sounds crazy," she replies, struggling through tears. "After everything that happened with B, Granny and I got into a heated discussion, and she brought it to my attention. She assumed I knew the man Nariah killed was my father, but I'd had no idea."

This has got to be a new and improved episode of *Punk'd,* and The Rock or Vin Diesel is about to come out and break the news because they know I would break Ashton in half playing with me like this. What the fuck is going on? Latavia and Nicole are sisters? I slept with and fell in love with—and proposed to—sisters? This is some bullshit!

Chapter Forty-nine

Nicole Is Blindsided

"Holy shit! I wish I'd been late to this damn appointment."

"Nicole, what's going on?"

"Dr. Bergman, is Darnell Carter one of your patients as well?"

"You know I cannot confirm or deny that question, Nicole. Let me ask you a question. If someone came into my office and asked the same question in relation to you, would you want me to answer them?"

"Of course not."

"So why would you think it would be okay for you to question if someone else may or may not be a patient of mine?"

"I apologize, but I just ran into him coming out of the building, and we shared some information with one another and . . ."

"Oh, my goodness, are you okay?" Dr. Berman questions as she grabs the wastebasket to help me vomit inside it.

"I am not and I apologize."

"Take some time and go into the restroom to clean yourself up. There's a new toothbrush in the cabinet and some toothpaste. Get yourself together, and we can talk when you're done."

"Are you okay to continue with our session, Nicole?"

"Yes, I am."

"Do you want to tell me what happened that has you so upset?"

"As I mentioned a minute ago, I was on my way in, and I ran into my ex-fiancé, Darnell. He is married to Latavia, the woman I recently found out is my half sister. Well, I mentioned to him I wanted to speak with his wife, and when he fought against it, it slipped out that she's my sister. Without question, he didn't believe me, so I broke it down to him how I found out and confirmed it was in fact very true. As we talked, I got a little upset because I felt he and his wife were responsible for my father's death no matter who killed him. Then—"

"Take your time, Nicole. If this is too much, we can take a little break. However, I feel you are very close to a breakthrough," she counsels me, handing me some tissues.

"I want to get this out because I'm going to lose my mind if I don't."

"You should thank God you didn't grow up around that bastard."

"How dare you speak ill of my father like that?"

"Look, sometimes God allows things to happen to us we don't understand. It may hurt in the beginning, but all in all, nine times out of ten, He is protecting us from something."

"So you're saying God protected me from growing up with a father to destroy my life in the long run?"

"*Listen, you have no idea what that man put my wife through. He was no father! He was a child-abusing pedophile, and you should thank your lucky stars you dodged that bullet.*"

"*What?*"

"*I'm sorry you had to find out like this, Nicole, but he was a monster,*" he apologized, moving in closer to hug me.

"*Don't touch me, you lying bastard! I hate you!*"

"After our confrontation, I ran away from him. I heard him over my shoulder saying he was sorry and he needed to get home to his wife, as if I give two shits about him or his wife."

"How do you feel about this information, and why are you so upset with Darnell?"

"I feel like the scum of the earth. Both of my parents were selfish, sick individuals, and they gave birth to a sick child who used her vagina to conquer and create a world of her own."

"You aren't sick, Nicole. You are a woman working through her pain who is on the verge of a breakthrough."

"The only thing I want to break through is my fist through someone's face."

"Where will that get you?"

"I don't know, but what I do know is I am sick of your questions. I'm out of here."

Chapter Fifty

Ramona's Mission

Ever since I found out about Delvin stepping out on me, I have been doing a lot of thinking about my childhood and my parents in particular. Just thinking about them has me on one because my mom put up with so much from my dad. You would think because he was a well-known pastor she would have had it easy. I truly believe that lifestyle is a myth and a fairy tale because Mom endured the complete opposite. The straw that broke the camel's back for me was when I witnessed my dad's "sister" getting off the floor after putting in some knee service in his office. I've despised that woman ever since.

Aunt Jeanie Langhorn, my dad's "sister," rebelled against my grandparents, and they put her out. They were very old school and lived by every letter, page, chapter, and period of the Bible. According to my dad, there were two lines from the Book of Joshua in particular—from 24:15—that they lived by and were their foundation: "Choose you this day whom ye will serve . . . But as for me and my house, we will serve the Lord."

Long story short, Aunt Jeanie was molested by one of the deacons in the church, and Granddad Langhorn said his duty as a man of God and a man of the cloth was to forgive, as that's what the Bible instructs. In other words, Aunt Jeanie had to attend church, eat dinner, and grow up around Deacon Timmons—the man who had violated her sacred places more than once. However, when she was old enough, she rebelled religiously, and when she was 16, my grandparents put her in a group home, which she ran away from.

She raised herself in the streets using drugs and alcohol as a scapegoat and selling her body to finance her habit of choice. What had brought her to our humble abode was when her john beat her so badly she was unrecognizable. My dad was listed as her next of kin. Like Granddad Langhorn, he had to do his due diligence as her "brother" and a man of the cloth, and he moved her into our home. At first it was great because she was the big sister I'd never had, and the stories she shared were mind-blowing. Well, our little sisterhood came to a screeching halt after I questioned her about her little prayer session with Dad.

"Aunt Jeanie, can I ask you a question?"

"Anything, sweetie."

"Are you and my dad biological brother and sister?"

"Of course we are. Why would you ask such a thing?"

"Well, I saw something today in his office. I know I don't have any siblings around anymore, but I know brothers and sisters don't do to each other what I saw you doing to my dad."

"I think you're mistaken. Your father was praying for me. I have a lot of things I'm dealing with, and his prayers always get answered for me."

"I know what I saw, Aunt Jeanie."

"What's your fresh ass doing knowing about sex anyway?"

"I never said you two had sex, Aunt Jeanie."

"Watch your grown-ass mouth before I slap you in it. Wait a minute, what do you know about sex anyway?"

"Never mind. I know I'm not crazy."

"We will see what your father has to say about you making up stories."

I bet we will see what he has to say. I'm sure we won't be running any of this by my mom.

Recapping all of that is a sure reason why I need to get myself together and make things right with Delvin. I refuse to be another statistic in my family by failing at my marriage. Since I'm near the mall, I will go into Frederick's of Hollywood to pick up something sexy and plan a nice, romantic evening. Since we have house guests, I will wear my little outfit home under a trench coat and lure him to a hotel suite that I will reserve for the weekend.

That's a good idea, if I do say so myself. I haven't lost it at all. I will show my husband exactly what he's been missing. He will think twice before he sniffs another woman.

In and out of the mall in record time, I am able to dip off by Elite to shower and change, and I am now flying home. I haven't been this excited in a very long time. I'm actually extremely horny, too. Delvin is in for a treat. He'd better have had his Wheaties this morning because he's going to need all the energy in the world for me. This is so long over—

Oh, my God, why is the ambulance at my house? That looks like Latavia on the stretcher.

"Darnell, what happened to her?" I quiz through tears as he boards the ambulance.

"She fell—"

"What? How? She was complaining about feeling lightheaded and was struggling to catch her breath the other day. It can't be because of that, can it?"

"We will meet them at the hospital, Mona," Delvin interjects.

This is god-awful. There has to be a black cloud over that poor woman. She is always going through something, and something is always happening to her.

Dear God, please cover and protect Latavia and that baby. Amen!

Chapter Fifty-one

Martinez's Heartache

Visions of Peterson's corpse haunt my mind like a plague. I can't seem to get the vision of his lifeless body and his wife holding my piece out of my head. I've already popped four pills, and they aren't working. I need to head on over to the liquor store. It's still early in the afternoon, so I should be good by the time I have to pick Gabby up. In fact, since it's Friday, I think I'll see if Granny wants to keep her for the weekend.

Yeah, that's a great idea. I'll blame it on work and throw the ol' lady a couple of dollars for her kindness, even though she won't accept it.

"Hey, Granny. How's it going?" I question when she answers on the first ring.

"I can't complain, Marty. How are you doing?"

"Pretty good. I wanted to know if you'd mind keeping Gabby for the weekend. I've been asked to do a double."

"Sure thing, Marty. I will square a few things away so we can have a girls' weekend. Don't work too hard, Marty, and make sure you eat and keep yourself hydrated."

"Yes, ma'am, and thank you."

That was easy, I think, closing my eyes to thank God. Oh, shit! I almost hit that woman. What the hell am I doing closing my eyes while driving? Is that Cola? It is. Damn, I almost ran over the love of my life—who I hate!

"Cola, you're going to get yourself killed if you don't get out of the damn road!" I yell out the window, which falls on deaf ears, because she keeps walking down the middle of the street.

"Leave me be. I'm better off dead."

"You're talking nonsense. Get in this car," I demand, exiting the car to assist her in getting in.

"Why do you care whether I live or die? I have been nothing but dishonest and unfaithful to you."

"That's no reason to wish death on you."

"I'm so sorry, *papi.* I miss you . . . I miss us."

"Believe it or not, I'm sick without you in my life."

I lean in closer to kiss her, but she pushes me back before asking, "What in God's name has you blasted out of your mind? Whatever it is, I want some!"

"I had a little to drink earlier, that's all. I was on my way to replenish. Would you like to take a ride with me?"

"I could use the escape, yes. But I know how you look with alcohol, and I can't trace that look, so cough it up. Whatever it is that has you dazed, I need some so I can meet you wherever you are right now mentally."

"Look, I hurt myself on the job, so I have some pain meds to ease the pain. I'm not supposed to drink with them, but sometimes I do. It's nothing."

"Well, I want some of nothing too. I have a lot of pain that needs to be eased as well."

"You want to talk about it?"

"I don't want to kill your buzz talking about me finding out my father is Latavia's father, the same man who sexually abused her."

"You're right. Let's save the chitchat for another time."

This is a bad idea. I should take her to her car and be on my way, but I miss her, and I miss us also. I think I need her right now. If I keep her by my side this weekend, maybe we can rekindle things. I don't know. I guess we can play it by ear. God, she smells so damn good. I could eat her alive. Maybe after we get back from the store, I'll do just that. I'm a little famished, too.

"What are you thinking about over there? Earth to *papi,* earth to *papi.*"

"I love it when you say that shit. Say it again," I beg, pulling her closer to me as I shove my tongue down her throat.

"What is that you put in my mouth?"

"You said you want to go with me, so let's go."

"So you store the shit in your mouth?"

"I was sucking on it until I picked up some gin, but I ran into you. Well, almost ran into you."

"I like this side of you, *papi.* You're turning me on."

"Is that right?"

Pulling up to Wine & Spirits, I get out real fast and grab three bottles of 1.75 liter, 80-proof bottles of gin. If I have it my way, we will have a very long weekend, and we need to be ready. Entering the car, I open the bottle and take a swig.

"I want some too."

"You sure?"

"Positive."

As she takes her swig, I reach over and recline her seat. I can't wait until we get home, and to make it easy for me, she has on a dress. *There is a God!* Now that she's in the perfect position, I position the top of my body over to her side of the passenger seat so it appears I'm looking for something.

"Excuse me, I need to get something from under here," I lie.

Like magic, she separates her legs, allowing me room to put my face between her legs. I am sort of upside down, but I position myself well enough so I'm face-to-face with her chocolate vault. Sliding my tongue through the side of her panties, I'm able to taste her creamy chocolate pudding, and I'm in heaven.

"Climb into the back seat so I can bury my face in it."

"Don't you want to wait until we get to your place?"

"No. Get in the back and lose those panties."

"Damn, *papi*."

Chapter Fifty-two

Delvin's Surprise

Fuck! What am I going to do? I have to think fast. There's no way I'm allowing this bitch to ruin my marriage. Bingo! The tape!

"Yo, my man, before the ambulance arrives, we need to get our stories straight. Your wife fell or the tape goes to the po—"

"Fuck you!" Darnell interrupts with a quick jab to my face.

"I'll let you have that, but that will be the last time you touch me, or your precious whore will go away for mur—"

Catching me again with another right hook to the side of my face, Darnell hisses, "Fuck you!"

Before I can react or respond, the sound of the sirens distracts me. I can hear the ambulance outside. Damn, they arrived in record-breaking time! I called them not even five minutes ago. Just my luck, as soon as we get to the truck, Mona comes frantically running up the driveway. This can't be good. I have no idea what this clown is going to say.

"Darnell, what happened to her?" Mona asks through tears.

"She fell—" the clown responds before getting cut off by another question from Mona.

Thank you, God. He fell for it and didn't say anything to Mona.

"What? How?"

"We will meet them at the hospital, Mona," I interject.

"Delvin, how did she fall? She doesn't look awake."

"I'm not sure, sweetheart. All I know is she fell and passed out."

"This is horrible!"

"It is, but I'm sure she will be fine. Don't pregnant women pass out a lot?"

"What kind of question is that?"

"I'm just trying to look on the brighter side. I hate seeing you upset."

"Thank you, but it isn't working."

I know what is working—my dick. Mona smells delicious, and those pumps she has on are sexy as fuck. I want to see them in the air.

"Mona?"

"Yes?"

"Can I ask you a question?"

"Sure, what is it, and can you drive a little faster please?"

"Yes, I can, but why do you have on that coat? It isn't that cold out."

"Oh, my Lord! I didn't get to change my clothes. It was a surprise for you."

"You mean to tell me you have nothing on under there?"

"Yes, I have this on," she replies, revealing a purple sexy outfit with the stockings and those straps.

Damn, I want to pull this car over, but I know she would kill me if I do. "Well, you look sexy as hell. I hope I get the chance to peel it off you later."

"How can you think about sex at a time like this, Delvin? I know I've been distant, but once all of this is over, I promise to make it up to you."

"Thank you, baby, for not giving up on us."

"How could I? I love you too much to just let go. We need to go to some kind of counseling because we can't ever come back here again."

Chapter Fifty-three

Darnell's Living Nightmare

"This has got to be a nightmare and I haven't woken up yet."

This has to be the worst fucking day in history. I ran into Nicole, who just so happens to be Latavia's sister. Delvin's punk ass tried to rape my wife, and now my wife is in this damn hospital, unconscious. To make matters worse, this man had the audacity to threaten my wife's freedom after what he tried to do to her. I will snap his fucking neck.

Let me calm down. Latavia needs me right now, but I will get that punk one way or the other. Why are the doctors taking so long to let me know what's going on with my wife?

"Mr. Carter?"

"Yes, Doctor, I am Mr. Carter."

"Hello, I am Dr. Givens. Your wife is being admitted to intensive care and has been given drugs. She is now stabilized. She suffered a minor stroke and slipped into a coma."

"A stroke? What? How? She didn't have any heart problems. Are you certain it was a stroke?"

"Yes, it was a stroke. It appears she has pneumonia. Do you know if she is being treated for it? Did she say she was ill at any point?"

"No. I know she had a cold and a minor cough, but nothing alarming that I know of."

"Sorry to interrupt. I'm her friend Mona, and she started complaining about feeling lightheaded and struggling to catch her breath for the past few days. She said she would contact her doctor today if it continued. Will she be all right? How is the baby?"

"Mrs. Carter was showing signs of premature labor and was given magnesium sulfate. This medication is given to women who are less than thirty-two weeks pregnant. The medication assists with preventing problems that can affect the baby's brain. In case of an emergency, we will need you to sign this consent giving permission to deliver the baby should the pre-term labor persist."

"This can't be happening," I sob, scribbling my name on the forms.

"I am so sorry, Darnell. We will get through this," Mona consoles me.

"Yeah, man. We are so sorry and will be here for you every step of the way."

"Get the fuck out of my face! This is your fault, you raping bastard!"

"Rape? Darnell, please let him go. You're going to kill him. Someone please come and help! He's going to kill my husband!"

"Sir, I'm going to have to ask you to calm down, or I'll have you escorted out of here," the flashlight cop threatens.

"No need. I'll do everyone a favor. I'll leave."

"Delvin, please don't go. Now is not the time. Let's talk about this."

"You stay here with your people. I'll see you when you get home."

"Please wait for me outside, Delvin."

"It's best he leaves before I hurt him, Mona. I'm sorry you're in the middle of this bullshit."

"Well, do you mind telling me why you nearly choked my husband to death and why you accused him of rape?"

"I think it'd be best if he told you that. He's a sick man is all I'll say."

"This doesn't make sense. Can you please tell me what happened, Darnell? I'm begging you."

"Look, I'm sorry. When I leave here, I will make arrangements to have our stuff removed from your home. Your husband tried to rape my wife, and I got there just in time."

"There has to be a mistake. Delvin is a lot of things, but a rapist isn't one of them."

"I know what I saw, Mona, and I am sorry you had to find out this way."

"So you're telling me you saw my husband, Delvin James Michaels, attempting to rape your wife, and she's in this hospital and not him?"

"I didn't physically see it, but I heard her yelling! Look, that's what happened, and my wife has no reason to lie, Mona."

"I didn't marry a rapist, Darnell. Something isn't adding up here."

All of this is like an episode of *Jerry Springer*. I feel like I am in the Twilight Zone or something. I don't understand it and can't explain any of this. My wife and I have traded places, and now she's in a coma. Isn't that ironic? Delvin tried to hurt her, and for what? He has a beautiful, smart wife of his own. From the looks of it, she was coming home to make up for lost time. I saw the net stockings when she sat down and her coat fell to the side. Latavia is the poster child for trench coats and sexy lingerie, so I knew what it was when I saw Mona. Either way, this day just can't get any worse. Where is Martinez? I've left him four messages, and I haven't heard a word from him.

Chapter Fifty-four

Nicole's Sexual Healing

Running into my *papi*—or almost getting run over by him after leaving Dr. Bergman's office—is and was the best thing that could have happened to me. I feel like a whole other person. Between the sex, alcohol, and pretty pills, we are having the best weekend ever. The sex is at an all-time high, too. This man cannot get enough of this chocolate pudding, and God knows I can't get enough of him. Speaking of the Energizer Bunny, here he comes for another dose of chocolate. My God, he's nibbling on my toes!

"Hey, baby girl, I think you need to check yourself out. While I was cleaning myself, I noticed some blood when I wiped off. Are you on your period?" he asks between nibbles.

Completely mortified as my buzz dies, I reply, embarrassed, "I just had it a couple of weeks ago."

"Well, it looks like she's back. Go check for yourself, beautiful."

No matter how sweet he tries to make it sound, this is humiliating. Of all times, how and why is this happening now? I slither the walk of shame to the bathroom, feeling like the scum of the earth. The bathroom is literally six footsteps from the bed, but it feels like a mile away. Grabbing the washrag, I clean myself as tears fall from my face. Looking down at the cloth, I realize there isn't a trace of blood. *Is he going crazy?*

"Oh, my God!" I blurt, running out of the bathroom.

"Are you okay, baby girl?"

"Ummmm, I'm not bleeding, so that means you busted my cherry. Does this mean after all the sex I've engaged in, I finally got my cherry popped at thirty-one?" I clown as we erupt in laughter simultaneously.

"Well, let me see if there's a cherry tree up in there I can take down."

"Damn, *papi,* I love when you talk like that," I purr as he pulls me closer to exchange saliva along with the three pills he leaves in my mouth as we break our kiss.

"We need to take this show to the great outdoors and spice this shit up. Here, take this bottle of gin. We're going to need it for our ride over. And one more thing . . ."

"What's that?"

"I want to spice this shit up. Let me blindfold you."

"Your wish is my command."

The curiosity is eating away at me. Where is he taking me? This is so exciting. I am literally blindfolded, can't see a thing, sipping on gin, and I feel amazing.

Distracting me from my one-woman show, he says, "We're here, baby girl. I'll take it from here. All you have to do is follow my lead."

"Yes, sir."

As he leads the way, holding my hand and stealing kisses in between, I am getting aroused with each step we take and the kisses. This is so what I need right now. I might need another pill or drink to combat the eerie feeling I'm having. It's probably the side effects of all the pills we've been popping along with the bottle of gin we've already demolished. Well, it must be wearing off, because a strange, spooky feeling comes over me, and I need to numb that mess right now.

"*Papi,* I think I need another dose of those pretty pills."

"Pretty pills?"

"Yes, pretty pills, because they make me feel pretty on the inside and the outside, and everything around me is just so pretty."

"You're beautiful, baby girl, and you don't need any pills to justi . . ."

"What's going on? Why did you stop talking? Should I remove my blindfold?"

"Everything is perfect. I just had to locate our destination, and that stays on until we leave, baby girl," he explains, throwing his tongue down my throat and leaving a couple of pretty pills in my mouth, allowing his hands to wander in my secret garden.

Thank heavens I don't have any panties on. Easy access for papi.

Taking me by his free hand, he pulls me in closer to him until our bodies become one. By reflex, I wrap my arms around his neck as he lifts my left leg above his hip. In order to maintain my balance, I wrap my leg around the back of his thigh.

"What are you doing to me, *papi?*"

Whispering seductively, he moans, "Just follow my lead. I promise you'll love every minute of it."

"Oh, my God," I whimper as he uses his tool to switch places with his fingers, entering me gently, thrusting in and out as I manage to keep my balance like a champ. "This feels so good, *papi.*"

"You're so wet. Damn, baby girl," he growls.

I don't know what it is, but this position is hitting all my spots, and every movement causes his pubic bone to rub up and down on my clit, triggering my chocolate lava to erupt all over him. I think this is the third orgasm. "Oh, my God, *papi,* I'm cum–"

"Fuuuuuck! This pussy is so good," he grunts as we reach euphoria at the same time.

"That was amazing, *papi.*"

"I'm not done. Turn around and bend over."

"How about I get on all fours for you, daddy?"

"That's even better. Assume the position, little momma."

Still blindfolded, I follow his lead down and can feel we're on the grass next to something hard and cold like concrete.

"Where do you have me? I want to see now. The mystery is getting me wet all over again."

"Keep it that way," he demands, ramming himself back inside my honey love.

"What are you doing to me?" I wail, climaxing as soon as he enters me.

"Treating you like you want to be treated," he snarls, removing my blindfold.

"I'm cumming again, *pa* . . . Oh, my God, get off of me! Why are we at a cemetery? Are you crazy?"

"You enjoyed yourself, didn't you?"

Looking down at the headstone, I can feel my stomach drop to my feet as I read the name of the deceased—WALTER WATKINS.

"You are a sick man! I just had an orgasm on my father's grave site."

"Multiple actually."

Chapter Fifty-five

Ramona Is Confused

There isn't a chance in hell I believe my husband tried to rape Latavia. Let's not forget she's pregnant. I refuse to believe Darnell. There has to be a misunderstanding. None of this makes any sense at all. He tried to rape her? Then someone please tell me what happened for her to end up in the hospital. I will ask my husband myself as soon as I get into that car. This elevator is taking forever to reach the lower level.

It's about time. Thank God, I think as the elevator bell rings, alerting me that I've reached the parking garage.

"Are you okay, baby? Did he hurt you?" I interrogate him as soon as I get the car door open.

"I'm fine, Mona. Let's get out of here. You know your friends are no longer welcome in my home?"

"Our home."

"You know what I mean."

"Do you mind telling me what that was all about?"

"I don't want to talk about it now."

"Well, that's not an option. I won't stand in the dark in my marriage any longer. Either you tell me the truth, or the Carters won't be the only ones not allowed in your home. You won't be either. Now get to talking."

"I'm sorry, Mona. You are the love of my life. I would never do anything to hurt you. You know it's been a long time since we've been intimate. I almost gave in to temptation."

"What the hell do you mean, you almost gave in to temptation? What happened, Delvin? And don't you dare lie to me!"

"Look, I'm sorry. I don't want to hurt you, but Latavia isn't the person you think she is. She came on to me. When she heard her coward come in the house, she started yelling and told him I tried to rape her."

"She came on to you? How?" I sob.

"Please stop crying, Mona. I know I messed up in the past, but I would never do anything to hurt you ever again. I swear!"

"Why would Latavia come on to you? She has her own husband."

"She mentioned something about being tired of oral sex. She just needed something hard in her to take her stress away."

"That sounds like Nae, not Latavia."

"Well, they say birds of a feather . . ."

"I don't know what to believe."

"Start by giving us another chance and believing the man you vowed to spend the rest of your life with. I am not your father, Mona. I know I messed up before, and I apologize. I will never betray you again, I swear. Please forgive me," he pleads as a single tear flees his right eye.

"I love you, Officer Michaels."

"I love you more, Mrs. Michaels."

Tomorrow I'll go by the nursing home and visit Mom. She and I need to have a heart-to-heart because I'm lost.

She's been in this situation time and time again with Dad. I know she'll know how to handle this. In the meantime, I'll work on repairing my marriage. There's no way I can allow myself to follow the trend of every other woman in my family and end up in divorce court.

"Are you all right over there, Mona?"

"Yes, I am. I was just thinking."

"About?"

"Well, we can't let this outfit go to waste. What can you do to make me take if off?" I flash him.

"Damn, baby, I thought you'd never ask. I'm driving as fast as I can to get you home."

"I don't want to go there. Let's do something spontaneous, like get a room for the night. Going home will just make me think too much and ruin the mood."

"I like the sound of that."

"Can we stop and get something to drink?" I purr as he rubs his hand up and down my thigh.

"Are you thirsty? What would you like? Water, juice, or one of those green smoothies you're always drinking?"

"Maybe something stronger, like vodka or that dark stuff you drink."

"Are you serious? You don't drink. You can't even handle the one glass of wine you religiously have on your birthday, our anniversary, special occasions, and holidays. So how is it that now you want to drink what I'm drinking?"

"Well, this is a special occasion. How long has it been for us?"

"It has been too long, in fact, but I don't want drunk pussy. I want my wife the way she came to me when I got her."

"Right now, you're ruining things, Delvin. Honestly, a drink will help me not think about everything that's going on." I brush my hand along the side of his face. "So either you're stopping or we're going home. The choice is yours," I conclude.

Chapter Fifty-six

Martinez Has Had Enough

Now she wants to give me the silent treatment. We were having a good time, and she wants to ruin it by getting caught up in her feelings. Hell, the man didn't give two shits about her, and he raped her sister. What better way to get back at him than to bust a nut on his grave site? We should have pissed on it, too. I was doing her a favor. I guess I went too far. Let me try to make it up to her since she's already ruined both of our highs.

"Cola, I apologize. I thought getting back at that bastard would make you feel better."

"How in God's name would taking me to a cemetery and having sex on top of my father's tombstone make me feel better, Martinez?"

"Now I'm Martinez?"

"That was the scariest and craziest thing I have ever done or witnessed. I am so scared of death, and you take me there of all places? Why would you do something so heartless and cruel?"

"Cruel is what that coward did to you and your sister!"

"You have no right to pass judgment. You should have allowed me to handle things my way."

"I almost ran into you when you were trying to handle things your way, and I saved you from yourself."

"I don't like the person you've become. Please take me home. I don't want to see your face ever again. Just wait until I tell Granny about your drinking and drugging. You will have the fight of your life to get Gabby from her."

"What you need to do is calm the fuck down!"

"Don't talk to me like that! I'm not afraid of you."

"Just shut up. I feel a little funny, and I don't need you in my ear right now."

"Take me home, and you won't hear me in your ear ever again!"

"Please shut up, Nicole!"

"Oh, my God. I asked you to take me home. Why are we back at your place?" she whines, storming out of the car.

"Woman, please!" I scold her, holding my chest.

"I hate you! I hate you!" she yells, banging on the hood of the car.

"Stop! You know what? Get in the car. I'm taking your crazy ass home!"

"Crazy? I've got your crazy!" she rants, pounding on the hood of the car.

If I didn't feel sick, I would run her annoying ass over and suffer the consequences. I don't need this shit. "Grab your shit out of the house and let's go."

"You don't have to tell me twice."

Maybe I overdid it. My head is spinning, I have pain in my chest, I am lightheaded, I'm sweating like crazy, and I can't breathe. Cola needs to hurry up. I don't know what's happening to me.

"Pop the trunk so I can put my things in there. I collected every stitch of clothing I had in that hellhole. What are you doing, sleeping? Pop the trunk. Why is the car moving backward? Stop playing! Oh, my God, stop the car!"

Chapter Fifty-seven

Delvin Is Caught Up

I hate lying to Mona, but there isn't a chance in hell I'm going to allow that cunt and her coward of a husband to ruin things for me and my marriage. Yes, I fucked up and had it bad for Nariah, but she's gone now. I can work on me and mine. One thing is for sure—I'm staying far away from these bipolar-ass women as well. How could Latavia accuse me of rape when she threw the pussy at me? I did what any other man would do and caught that shit.

Damn, she reminds me of Nariah so much it's sickening. Every time I was with Latavia, it was like I was having an out-of-body experience. It was as if she'd transformed into Nariah and was able to give me something my wife will never be able to give me—a baby. In my mind, she was Nariah carrying my baby, which was the only way I was able to do anything with her. I tried to knock Mona up just like I tried to knock Nariah up, but Mona can't have children due to some surgery she had as a child or something. If Nariah were still here, she would be carrying my baby, I promise you that.

Well, enough reminiscing. She's no longer with us, and my wife is in the restroom right now freshening up for me. In fact, what the hell is she doing in there?

"Mona? Is everything all right in there?"

"Yes, this vodka has me stuck on the floor. Can you please come help me?" she chuckles.

Opening the bathroom door to find my wife drunk on the floor is the last thing I want to do right now. "What are you doing, and why did you take that bottle to the head? You know you can't handle alcohol like that, Mona."

"I was just trying to make the pain go away so I could be all you need me to be. I don't want you to end up breaking my heart any more than you already have," she slurs.

"I've already apologized to you over and over again, and you're still hanging on to that shit, Mona!"

"Don't you dare talk to me like that, Delvin! I don't curse at you. I refuse to allow you to be disrespectful and curse at me."

"Look, I apologize. I didn't mean to talk to you like that. I am begging your forgiveness for me stepping out on us. Nariah is gone, and what she and I shared left with her, so please let's move past it."

"So . . . if she were still here . . . you would still be sharing? Is that what you're saying to me right now?"

"No! You know what I meant."

"Honestly, I don't. Please elaborate."

"What do you mean?"

"If she were still alive, would you still be sharing whatever it is you shared with her?"

"Of course not, Mona! I screwed up that one time and will never allow anything or anyone else to come between us."

"Can I ask you another question?"

"Of course you can," I reply, dreading this whole conversation and her badgering, which I know is up next.

"What was it she had that I don't have? Do you not find me attractive anymore? Am I unable to please you like I used to? Are there any other women I should know about? Oh, my God, do I need to be tested?"

"Mona, please calm down. There will never be another woman. You are the perfect fit for me. God handcrafted you just for me. Just like Eve was Adam's perfect fit, and the same way Eve messed up, I messed up."

"That's the same line my daddy used to use on my momma when he was lying. Please tell me you aren't like my daddy. Please, Delvin. Please!"

"Trust me, I am nothing like your father. There isn't and never will be anyone else. I love you and only you, Mona. You are my rib."

Taking another swig of her poison, she garbles, "Show me just how much I mean to you, and make love to me."

"I don't want you like this, Mona. Lie down for a little while and sober yourself up first."

"No, I want you now! Take your penis out."

"What?"

"Take it out," she says, stumbling toward me, grabbing at my belt buckle. I can't believe she is this drunk. This is such a turn-off for me.

"You aren't even hard. Can I kiss it to make it better?"

"This is not you, Mona, and I don't like seeing you like this."

"Just put it in my mouth and stop whining."

"Stop it!"

"If I were Nariah, I bet you wouldn't hesitate. I can't even get an erection from you anymore or turn you on. What's wrong with me? I thought you loved me," she wails.

What the fuck is going on? Just looking at my wife, my dick is usually inflated, especially in the little getup she has on. Something must be wrong with me. Maybe I need to get checked out. This is some bullshit!

Chapter Fifty-eight

Darnell's Nightmare Continues

"It's extremely difficult for me to come to grips with the man I've become. Now that I'm thinking about it, maybe I've always been this way and I've just done a hell of a job concealing my true identity. Shortly after the services for my boy Nard, I noticed a shift in my behavior, and I became enraged and irritable all the time. For instance, instead of confronting my wife like a real man, I allowed my anger and disappointment to fester, which catapulted me into taking every chance I could to belittle her, along with pushing and shoving the woman I'd professed to love for the balance of my life.

"When this rage hits me, it's as if I take on a sudden case of tunnel vision and my brain wiring stops clicking all at once. I just see black and snap. This last incident was probably the worst and the reason why I'm here with you today. See, it has been a few weeks, or more like a month, since Latavia and I have been intimate. We still haven't had actual intercourse since before my accident. Oral communications have been our intimate and sexual language. Out of nowhere, that came to a complete halt.

"Latavia covered it up, saying, 'My love, this baby is draining the life out of me. I can't believe my desire for *sex has suddenly evaporated.' Well, that might be what she verbalized, but what I heard her say was, 'Because I'm pregnant with my first love's child, I no longer need or want you,' and that's when I lost it. I became furious, and something snapped in me, ushering me over to where she was lying on the bed. I climbed on top of her and sat all of my body weight on top of her loaded pregnant stomach."*

"*If you've never done anything like this before, what would you say is the root of your actions? Where did this angry, aggressive, and abusive behavior stem from?*" *Dr. Bergman cross-examines.*

"Mr. Carter? Mr. Carter?" Dr. Givens summons.

A little delirious and unsure as to where I am until I realize I was dreaming, I stutter, "Yes, yes. I apologize. I must have dozed off. Is everything all right with my wife?"

"She's stable. However, we weren't able to stop the pre-term labor and had to perform an emergency C-section."

"Jesus! How is my wife? How's the baby, Doc?"

"Both are stable. Your wife gave birth to a one-pound, ten-ounce baby girl. Because she gave birth at twenty-eight weeks, the baby won't be able to breathe on her own. We will have to put her on a breathing tube to assist her breathing. She will more than likely spend some time in NICU—"

"I'm sorry, Doc, but what is NICU?"

"I apologize. NICU stands for Neonatal Intensive Care Unit."

"Yes, you're right. I remember now. All of this has my mind all over the place."

"I can understand. Your little girl will remain in NICU until her lungs are fully developed and working and until she puts on a healthy weight gain, Mr. Carter."

"Thank you, Dr. Givens. When can I see them?"

"Mrs. Carter is in recovery. I will have a nurse come for you in a few. Your daughter should be set up in NICU downstairs on the fourth floor."

"Thank you for everything, Dr. Givens."

"You're welcome, Mr. Carter."

This shit just went from bad to worse. Where the hell is Martinez? I haven't heard a word from him. I don't think I can do this alone. Damn, I wish my boy were here.

Looking up to the ceiling, I silently pray. *I know I'm strong, but damn, God, can a brother get a break? You said you wouldn't put any more on us than we can bear, but I'm at my breaking point. Please don't let me lose my wife, God. I'll do whatever I have to do to make things right, God. Please don't take my wife away from me. She's all that I have left. I don't have anyone else, God. Please hear my prayer. Help me because I can't help myself at this point. I need you now, God. Amen.*

I guess I'll make my way downstairs to NICU and check on my . . . daughter? That actually makes my heart smile, considering. No matter what happens, I will love, protect, and raise this child as my own.

God, I have another favor. You brought this baby into our lives for a reason. Please look on her, and let her be all right. She's innocent in all of this, God. She didn't ask to be here or to be brought here under these circumstances. I vow to love, honor, and protect her in sickness and in health as I do my wife. Amen.

As soon as I reach the fourth floor, anxiety drapes my mind, and I have knots in my stomach. I have never done well with hospitals, and having my family in one is taking a toll on me. *Well, it's now or never,* I coach myself as I reach the nurses' station.

"Good evening. I'm the . . . parent . . . husband of Latavia Carter. Her . . . I mean, our baby girl was just brought down here."

"No problem. Right this way, Mr. Carter. We're just getting her settled. In the meantime, I want to bring you up to speed so you're comfortable with everything before going in, because it can be a little overwhelming at first."

"I understand."

"By the way, I'm the head nurse, Nurse Cullen, but you can call me Amy."

"Nice to meet you, Amy. I'm Darnell."

"Same here. Now before we go inside, I want to touch base with you."

"No problem at all."

"As you are aware, your wife gave birth to your daughter prematurely, and she wasn't finished growing. Therefore, your little girl won't look like a baby who was carried a full nine months. By the way, did you two have a name picked out for her yet?"

"I believe so, but my wife wasn't certain. Is it possible for us to wait for my wife to make that decision?"

"Of course it is. Right now, your daughter will be put in an enclosed, see-through plastic crib called an incubator. This special crib will keep her warm, and she won't need to be wrapped in blankets. She will also have a cap on her head so her head stays warm as well. The incubator is comprised to lessen the risk of an infection as well as control the moisture in the air to keep your baby from losing water. I know this is a lot. Please let me know if I'm going too fast. Do you have any questions so far?"

"No, I'm good."

"There will be tubes and wires attached to her, which can seem scary too, but they aren't hurting the baby. The tubes and wires are connected to monitors. They check the baby's breathing, heart rate, blood pressure, and temperature at all times."

I just want to go in and get this over with.

"That pretty much covers everything in a nutshell. Are you ready to go inside?"

"As ready as I'll ever be."

"If you have any questions, please feel free to ask. Your daughter is on the far left."

"Thank you, Amy."

"No problem at all. Either I or the doctor will be back shortly to give you an update on your daughter."

I can't even respond to her as tears stream down my face. It's like I'm staring at a miniature version of Latavia. Well, not all the way. She's so tiny she can fit in the palm of my hand. Her skin looks old and wrinkly. We will definitely have to fatten her up when she gets out of here.

"Excuse me, Nurse, how does she eat?" I quiz as one of the nurses approaches me.

"Good evening, Mr. Carter. The tube through her nose carries food to her stomach, and the other tubes bring fluids and medicine."

"Damn, this is too much."

"It can be, but you have to try to be strong for her. She needs you."

"Thanks. I will try my best."

All of this is entirely too much for one person to handle, but like Nurse Whatever-her-name-is said, I have to be strong for her and Latavia. Speaking of Latavia, I have to go see her next.

"God, I need your strength."

Chapter Fifty-nine

Granny Is Concerned

"Lord, I can feel it. Something isn't right. My grand-baby ain't been home, and Marty ain't bothered to call to check on this baby. Now you know, Lord, that ain't like him. Please, God, cover my grandbaby and Marty. I'm sick to my stomach over those two. They're both in a bad way and don't even know it. I know you separated them because they're no good to anyone right now, not even to themselves. Help my babies, Lord. They need your hand wrapped around them. Thank you in advance, dear Lord."

I think I have Darnell's number in my old wallet with all my numbers. I'm going to try him because something just ain't right. "Here it is," I nervously cheer, picking up the house phone to call. *I pray he still has the same number after all these years,* I think as the phone rings.

"Hello? Mrs. Neal? Is everything all right?" Darnell quizzes, answering the phone after only one ring.

"Yes, baby, I believe everything is fine. I put it in God's hands. How did you know it was me calling you after all these years, baby?"

"I'm a creature of habit. I've had the same phone—well, the same carrier—and number since I was twenty, Mrs. Neal, and I've kept all the numbers programmed in my phone."

"You always were ahead of your time. I just wish my grandbaby had known that before she messed over you and now Marty. Anyway, I'm calling because I can't seem to get a hold of my grandbaby or Marty. Have you seen or spoken to either of them?"

"Marty, Mrs. Neal?"

"William! You know who I'm talking about, boy!"

"I apologize, Mrs. Neal, but are you talking about Martinez? I've been trying to get a hold of him myself. I'm at the hospital right now, but I'll look into it and get back to you. Is that all right?"

"Hospital? Are you all right?"

"I hope so. I'm here with my wife. She had an accident and isn't doing well."

"Listen here, baby, you put her in God's hands. He's a healer. Do you hear me? He's a healer, and He can and will take care of your wife. You have to ask, believe, and receive it. Do you hear me? Don't give up. God didn't give up on you. You hang in there, and I'll be checking in on you later. Go on and tend to your wife. I love you, little boy. You hear me? I don't care what happened between you and my grandbaby. You will always be a son to me. You hear me?"

"Yes, ma'am, and thank you. I really needed to hear that. I feel like I'm all alone. My daughter is also in the hospital. She was born early and is barely hanging on to her life as well. This is too much for one person to handle, Mrs. Neal, but I am holding on."

"You have to stop trying to carry things God has His hands on. He has it under control, baby. I know it's easier said than done, but you have to let go and give your baby girl and your wife to God. They need you, Darnell, just as much as you need the Lord right now. He is your strength. Now hold on to Him. Do you hear me?"

"Yes, ma'am, and thank you."

"You're welcome, baby. Now go be the husband and father to your family God has blessed you to be. They will be all right. Just believe."

Lord, what is going on with these kids? If it isn't one thing, it's another. Help these babies, God. They're lost and making foolish choices, and it's coming back to get them. Lord, please be easy on these babies.

Let me go on and feed this baby and get myself under control. I am not a worrier, but these kids have got my pressure up. I can't get past this feeling. It's the same one I had when my Daniel passed. Lord, I remember that dreadful day like it was this morning. The devil sure was busy that day he took my beloved Danny away from me. We'd had a terrible fight that day over supper, which was the last time I spoke to my beloved.

Danny and I had been struggling a little as business at his shop was at an all-time low, causing him to be irritable all the time. We clashed every time we were together like two jealous schoolgirls. It was so bad that every time the number to his shop showed up on the caller ID, I tuned the phone out along with anyone who came knocking on the door. I had to learn about my husband's death on the evening news. I've canceled my cable subscription since.

Every time my mind travels back, all I can hear are the words of Sade Baderinwa as she reported. *"Breaking news: a man was killed this morning when a car he was working on fell and crushed him. The incident occurred around ten twenty-three a.m. Lieutenant Justin Howell of the Queens Police Department said the fifty-eight-year-old male was underneath a Ford Taurus and had removed the front passenger wheel to perform some work.*

The vehicle came off the jack for an unknown reason, and the man was crushed beneath the car. Police have identified the victim as Daniel Neal of Maspeth. Witnesses attempted to render emergency aid, but the man passed away. We'll have more on this tragic story as it unfolds. Tune in tonight at seven p.m. for more coverage."

"Lord, please take the pain away. I know you had need of my Danny, but I miss him so."

Chapter Sixty

Ramona Learns The Truth

I don't know what to believe anymore. Delvin is completely turned off by me. We have tried too many times to rekindle our flame in the bedroom. Unfortunately, I can no longer light his fire. I'm not sure what it is, but it is depressing. Since I don't have any major appointments or errands to run, I think I'll go visit Mom at the nursing home. Mom never speaks when I visit. She just sits in the recliner and stares straight ahead like she's hypnotized or something. I won't give up on her. No matter what, I visit and talk to her as if she's communicating right back with me. There is no one I could or would trust with the intimate details of my marriage, so I talk to Mom about it. Although she never responds, it always feels good to get it off my chest. I pray she's ready for the load I'm about to drop on her in the next five minutes considering I'm pulling up now.

I don't know why I allowed Delvin to talk me into putting my mom away in the first place. I am so disappointed in myself. Trying to make my marriage work blew up in my face. The joke is clearly on me.

"Hello, Mother. You're looking exceptionally vibrant today. You have a glow since I was here two days ago."

Of course that doesn't work. Guess I'll continue talking to myself.

Through tears I gush, "Mom, if there were ever a time I needed you, it's right now. Everything is a mess. I told you about what happened with Latavia and her husband and that they are now staying with Delvin and me. Well, now she's in the hospital fighting for her life. Her husband is accusing Delvin of raping her. My husband is no rapist. There has to be a misunderstanding, but Latavia isn't stable enough for me to question her. I don't know what to do, and to drive the knife in deeper, my husband lost his erection for me."

I can't believe I just told my mom about my husband's soft penis.

Looking up at my mom, I can see a single tear streaming down her face. "Mom, are you all right? Why are you crying?"

Grabbing my hand, she speaks softly. "The eyes, princess, the eyes."

"Your eyes, Mom? Something's wrong with your eyes? I will get a nurse for you," I yell, running toward the door as she continues to speak, stopping me in my tracks.

"His eyes will tell it all. It's the gateway to his soul, princess. Listen to his eyes."

Turning around to face her before I fall at her feet, I begin to wail. "He wouldn't look into my eyes when we spoke about it, and deep down inside, I could feel something wasn't right because of it."

"Listen to his eyes, princess. Don't make the same mistake I made," she instructs a little over a whisper.

"Mom, it isn't your fault Dad slept with all of those women. You loved him, and you blamed yourself for having Monty out of wedlock. I so wish Monty were still alive. I'm sorry for mentioning him," I apologize, seeing tears mask her face.

"There's so much you still don't know, princess, and I don't want you to hate me. I chose the life I led because I didn't know who I was. I was insecure, ashamed, and didn't think I would ever find true love because I was all used up."

"Don't talk like that, Mother. You didn't make Dad have all of those affairs with all those women in the church. Let's not forget his so-called sister either."

"Your father never slept with any of those women, Mona. He's done his dirt, but I know for a fact he never slept with any of those women."

"Mom, you're in denial. You and I both know he did."

"Listen to me and hear me good," she spoke sternly.

"Yes, ma'am."

"Your father was raped as a child by the same person who raped his sister, and because of that, he has never been with a woman intimately."

"All right, Mom. I can see you aren't well and you're delirious. I'll go see if the nurse can give you something."

Grabbing my wrist firmly, she continues to speak. "Sit down and listen to me. I should have shared this with you a long time ago. Maybe you wouldn't hate your dad so much and would actually go see him sometime. He loves you just as much as I do, if not more, Mona. You can't carry that hate in your heart. The same hate I have for myself you hold for your dad. You won't be able to prosper in your life or your marriage with a hardened heart, princess."

"Mom, you aren't making any sense, and you're scaring me."

"When your dad and I married, it was an arranged marriage. I was a single mother in the church, and because of my past, I was ashamed of myself and your brother. I didn't do anything except go to church. When I was home, I would read my Word or listen to it, day in and day out. I didn't have a social life at all. When your father came to me with a proposition, I couldn't resist. I thought agreeing to what he proposed would help me escape my past and embrace the woman I was supposed to be. But that was the devil playing on my insecurities, and the opposite happened."

"Arranged marriage? Proposition? What are you saying, Mother? Is Dad not my father?"

"Please let me finish. This is hard for me. I will answer all of your questions when I'm done, all right?"

"Yes, ma'am."

"I can recall our conversation like it was yesterday," she says with sadness in her eyes, tapping my hand for me to move to allow her to stand.

I haven't seen my mom get out of that chair in over four years. The nurses usually move her around. "Mom, do you need help?"

"It's about time I stand up for something, even if it took me all my life to do so. I refuse to sit in that chair another second and allow you to endure the same heartache I did. I spent all of my life in my own shadow, princess."

Tears parade down my caramel skin. Deep down inside I can feel this is going to be the toughest pill I've ever had to swallow.

"Your dad asked for my hand in marriage. I was overjoyed that he'd chosen me out of all the women in the church who threw themselves at him regularly. The downside of it was I had to agree to be loyal and faithful to him, knowing we would never bed one another—"

Cutting her off, I scream, "Mom, you aren't making any sense! How am I here if you two are my parents when you've never had sex?"

"Lower your voice, young lady. We went to the doctor to get you, princess. I'm so sorry you had to find out like this, and now of all times, when you're dealing with so much."

"So I'm adopted? Stolen? What are you saying, Mom? Please stop beating around the bush."

"No, your dad and I are your parents. We used this process called intrauterine insemination. It is a procedure the doctor performs in which he places a man's sperm inside a woman's uterus when she's ovulating, but in this case, your dad's sperm was used in order for us to conceive you, princess."

I've been in this bathroom stall staring at the door for almost an hour after running out of my mom's room. I cannot believe my parents never touched one another. Mom had the nerve to say Dad never slept with any of those women, or any woman period. This doesn't make sense at all. I think for the first time in my life I am fighting mad. *I want answers and I want them now,* I think, marching out of the restroom to confront my dear mother.

"Mom, I by no means would ever disrespect you, but I am completely confused. How is it possible that you and my dad never had sex, yet you were married for years? You two lived the perfect marriage outside of his wandering eye, hands, and other things. You've vacationed together and saved so many marriages! So please enlighten me how in God's name is any of what you're telling me possible?"

"I want you to remember how much your father loves you, Mona. No matter what his lifestyle is or was, he is still and will always be your father. He loves you with every fiber of his being."

"Mom, please answer me! Please."

"Your father had a thorn in his flesh just like Paul did in the Bible. When your dad was nine years of age, he was raped by a deacon in the church. Ever since then, he has craved the touch of a man. He has tried to fast and pray that spirit off him, but the harder he tried, the more aggressive the urge took over him."

"So, Mom, in other words, what you're saying is that my dad's a fag? Is that what you're telling me, Mom? My dad's a fag?"

"No, he is not, and don't ever disrespect him like that again, Ramona."

"How could you have covered this filth up all this time, Mom?"

"When we married, he confided in me and poured his heart out to me. We've undergone countless hours of counseling and had to go out of state to do so. No matter what we did, he couldn't kick that addiction or fight that demon off him."

"Why did you stay?"

"Believe it or not, I love your father, and I am in love with him. He is the first and only man who has treated me with the utmost respect and loved me unconditionally outside of God."

"Mom, love doesn't neglect its wife or its husbandly duties."

"That's what's wrong with your generation, princess. Sex isn't love. You think that because you have a good night in the sack he loves you? That won't stop a man from making another woman feel the same way that man made you feel. Love covers, love forgives and accepts. Real love knows your weaknesses and won't take advantage of them. It knows your flaws and still accepts you. That's love, princess."

"Mom, no disrespect, but from where I'm sitting, Dad used your weakness of being a single mother to take advantage of you."

"Shut your mouth. He did not force me into marrying him. I had a choice. From the moment I stepped foot in that church and felt the way he allowed God to use him to speak to those empty places in my life, I fell in love with him. I carry that love every day because he is a great, God-fearing man."

"He fears God so much and wants so much to be like God that he goes through men to feel God. Is that what you're saying, Mother?"

"You are not too old for me to slap your face, Ramona. I am not going to sit here and allow you to speak ill of your father. He knew he had a problem and tried to make love to me time and time again, but his organ had a mind of its own and wouldn't respond. It ate him up so badly. He finally gave me permission to find a male friend who he would screen and approve of to satisfy my sexual needs. However, I declined because my body belonged to your father and your father only."

"Mom, I can't believe what I'm hearing. It isn't adding up. Do you mind explaining what he was doing with his sister and the other women of the church? Did you two really go on vacations, or was that a lie as well?"

"We've never lied to you, princess. Instead, we covered you and protected you. When we went on vacations, your father would get two rooms so he could meet up with his friend. In the beginning, I hated it, but I prayed when he would leave the room that he would spend less time away from me. As far as the other women, oral sex is the only thing he would allow women to do to and for him while he was trying to overcome that demon that lived inside him. He said that my mouth was too precious, that he wouldn't allow me to disgrace myself like that."

"That's sick, Mom. You two hid behind the words in that Bible but never lived by it. How is that a marriage, and how in the world could you two counsel anyone when you are the ones who needed the counseling?"

"I just want you to move past this and forgive your father. He didn't put me in here. I put myself in here because my heart began to ache when he told me he loves me but is in love with his friend and wanted to move him into the basement apartment of our home."

"That's it! I have heard enough! Good night, Mom. I will come back to see you in a few days. I need some time."

Everything they'd taught me was a lie. I don't have a father. I have a sissy who cares for himself and himself only. Forgive him? Yes, I do, but he no longer exists in my eyes. Here I was walking around being the perfect daughter, abiding by the words my parents had instilled in me, and it was all a lie. My dad dishonors God by having a fascination with men's booty holes. Sickening! Just sickening.

Right now, I need to pull myself together. I don't want to see Delvin at the moment. I think I'll swing by the hospital to check on Latavia. Speak of the devil, there's Delvin calling me now.

"Hello?"

"Hey, babe, where are you?"

"Why?"

"I was just checking on you and wanted to know if you heard what happened."

"I was visiting my mom. What's wrong? Are you all right?"

"I'm fine, but your friends may not be. Martinez had a heart attack and died. It's all over the news."

Without responding, I disconnect the call. What in God's name is going on? Do these people have some kind of root on them? Everyone is either getting shot or stabbed, or dying. Jesus, give me the strength I need to be there for my friends.

Chapter Sixty-one

Delvin's Dilemma

All this time I have been waiting for my wife to come around and spread-eagle for me, and when the time comes, I can't perform. My Johnson won't even acknowledge her. What the fuck is going on with me? Maybe I need to check myself into a Nariah rehab. I can see it now: *hello, my name is Delvin Michaels, and I am a Nariaholic.* Yeah, I am most definitely slipping. In all of my 30-plus years, I have never been this open over a woman. I don't know what it was about her, but she had me spellbound, like some voodoo priestess or something.

Seriously, I love Mona with every fiber of my being. I just didn't know what to do to fix our relationship problems, so I stepped outside to fill in the holes—literally. If you process it, I cheated to save my marriage. I didn't fall out of love with my wife, I was just unsatisfied with the current state of our union. I suffered in silence and felt like less than a man, knowing that no matter what I did or tried to do, I couldn't stimulate my wife's sex drive. When Nariah came on to me, it made me feel on top of the world. I really thought my affair would help me help us because it did what I knew it would and awakened my sex drive. At the end of the day, Mona was always the woman I wanted the most and whom I feel most comfortable with sexually—or so I thought.

If I put my pride to the side for a second, I can and will admit I fucked up royally. Had I not messed with Nariah, there isn't a chance in hell I would have given Latavia a chance. Let me not forget the little number on the job I allowed to lure me into having sex. Come to find out it was a setup. I've been suspended indefinitely because of it. I should have known something was up, but I allowed my third eye to do the thinking for me when she bent over and displayed just how good her momma had been to her. This inmate kept throwing herself at me, just like Nariah had, every chance she got as soon as she locked eyes on me. For instance, at mealtime, I was standing at the door as usual when she walked past me and said, "Forgive me if I'm out of line, but I would love to see what you look like underneath that uniform."

"Is that right, inmate?"

"If not, I can make it just right for you, if you know what I mean."

"I guess you're going to have to show me just what it is you're saying."

That's all it took—along with the ghost of Nariah meeting us in there. I could actually feel her presence as soon as I entered the closet. That alone had me lock, stock, and barrel. Ten minutes later, she was on her knees, schooling me like she was the board of education and as if she were on a mission to be at the head of the class. As soon as her lesson was concluded, the warden's little snitch came knocking on the door, saying she heard noises coming from the closet that had alerted her.

How can I even attempt to explain that little fiasco to Mona? There's no way I can. I am going to have to do something until I can find something else. Fuck! No one will hire me with this shit on my record. In the meantime, I will play it cool. I still have another check due this week and my little "don't let the wife know" stash. Maybe I need some therapy behind all of this. I'm going to throw myself at the mercy of the warden to see if I can see someone in the hope that it will help me get my job back. Mona always says that nothing beats a failure but a try. I pray all of this will roll over smoothly without her catching wind of any of it.

Chapter Sixty-two

Darnell's Living Thunderstorm

I think I'll go downstairs and get me some water or something. My mouth is dry as hell. *Who am I fooling? I need a breather before I go see Latavia anyway,* I think with my eyes closed, resting my head on the wall as the elevator transports me to my destination.

"Darnell?" Mrs. Neal sings through tears.

"Yes, ma'am. What are you doing here? Are you all right?"

"No. Something's happened to Nikki and Marty."

Please tell me this is not happening right now. Afraid to hear her response, I ask, "What do you mean, something's happened to them?"

"Oh, Lord! Darnell, when Marty's neighbor got home, he saw the car on top of my grandbaby, and Marty was dead."

"Dead? No, that can't be! There's no way he's dead! Are you sure, Mrs. Neal?"

"Yes, baby. I had my neighbor carry me over to his place, and the medical people who took him in the ambulance pronounced him dead when they got there. That poor little girl doesn't have a mother or father now," she sobs.

"What about Nicole? Is she all right?"

"I'm not sure. She wasn't alert or conscious when they got to her. I'm headed down to the ER now. I don't think I can handle it if something happens to my grandbaby. Lord, you said you won't put more on me than I can bear," she prayed aloud.

I really don't know what's going on, but Martinez can't be dead. What the fuck is going on? Before I can gather my thoughts, my old sergeant boards the elevator as Mrs. Neal exits saying, "Darnell, I'll give you a call later. Go check on your wife and Marty. I will take care of Gabby like she's my own," she whimpers.

"Yes, ma'am," I reply with little to no emotion. I feel like I'm having the longest nightmare and can't wake up.

"Hey, Carter, sorry to hear about your wife. I'm sure you heard about Martinez."

"No, sir. I heard pieces, but I'm not clear on what happened."

"He's been out of it for a while and was on leave. Off the record, I think he was in a bad way."

"A bad way?"

"A few people said he hadn't been himself and swore he was using."

"That's bullshit! There's no way in hell Martinez would use anything! He despised drugs as much as I do, if not more."

"Well, we'll have to wait for the tox report. I know he was your friend, and I am sorry for your loss."

"Yeah, thanks."

He is sorry for my loss, like he didn't know him as well as I did. Yeah, it's good he got his inconsiderate ass off the elevator with me. I thought I was going to lose it.

Lord, what's really going on? I just can't go upstairs to see Latavia. I can't take anymore. I'm a man, and I'm standing here crying like a bitch, talking to you because I am at my breaking point. How could you allow this to happen? What did I do that was so bad that you had to take everyone I love away from me? I pray as I cry, dropping to my knees.

"Mr. Carter?" a male voice quizzes from behind me as he places his hand on my shoulder.

Not lifting my head to acknowledge or see who it is I'm speaking to, I mumble, "Whoever you are, please leave me be. I need to be alone right now before I lose it in here and end up behind bars. I can't take any more bad news. Please leave me the hell alone."

"I'm sorry, Mr. Carter, but I think you'll want to hear this."

"What is it?" I bark, standing and turning to face the voice I can now see belongs to Dr. Givens. "I apologize, Doc. What's up?"

"I have great news. Your wife is awake."

Chapter Sixty-three

Latavia Is Confused

Unsure as to where I am, I begin to panic, breathing very hard, causing alarms to go off. As nurses run to my bedside, it dawns on me that I am in the hospital. But how the hell did I get here?

"How are you feeling, Mrs. Carter?"

Yanking the tubes from my face, I try to tell the nurse that I think I'm okay, but I struggle with getting the words out. My mouth is moving, but no words are heard.

"Please hold on and take it easy. Your nurse, Miss Lucas, will be in here to help you. You really should have waited for us to remove everything," she scolds as she proceeds to check my vitals.

"Your husband is going to be so happy to see you up. We have photos of your little girl," Miss Lucas blurts out, shoving pictures of this plucked chicken–looking baby in my face as soon as she enters the room.

Still unable to verbalize my response, I shake my head in disbelief because I have no recollection of being pregnant. Yet this nurse is showing me all of these photographs of a baby I supposedly gave birth to. The last thing I remember is marrying the man of my dreams. Where is Darnell? Where is Nae? I so need both of them right now. I am so scared. What has happened to me?

"From the puzzled look on your face, I believe you're having a hard time with this. Don't worry, Dr. Givens went to find your husband. He should be in here shortly to speak with you. When your eyes opened and you were beginning to breathe on your own, Dr. Givens started the necessary treatments to wean you off, but it looks like you may have bypassed that step—"

"Oh, my God, Latavia, baby," Darnell cries as he enters the room with a visibly tearstained face.

"Darnell," I half mumble through tears.

"You scared me. I'm so glad and blessed to have you back. God knows I couldn't handle anything else happening."

"Mr. Carter, she's a fighter, and from the looks of things, she will pull through this," Dr. Givens notes. "We will run a series of tests to make sure we're in the clear with everything. In the meantime, Mrs. Carter, take it easy. I know your throat feels sore, but that will subside. Try to drink water, and take it easy."

"Thank you for everything you've done for my wife, Doc."

"You're welcome," he acknowledges before exiting the room.

"What happened to me?" I murmur in a raspy voice.

"You don't remember?"

"No, and the nurses showed me pictures of a baby."

"You mean to tell me you don't remember anything at all? Not even having a baby, Latavia?" he questions in an unfamiliar tone.

"I'm sorry, I don't, and it's scaring me."

"You don't remember leaving me in a hospital for a little over a month hanging on to my life while you re-kindled your high school romance and got knocked up? You're telling me you don't remember any of that, Latavia?"

"What? I would never do that to you, Darnell. What are you talking about?" I sob.

"Just like you didn't remember killing your father and allowing Nariah to take the fall for it? I supposed that's all a mystery to you as well?"

"Why are you speaking to me like that? I swear I don't remember any of that!"

"Is everything all right?" Nurse Lucas quizzes, barging back into the room.

"It appears my wife has amnesia and can't remember a long history of things that have happened in the last year or so. She doesn't recall being pregnant, among other things."

"Mr. Carter, after all she just endured, it is possible to have memory loss. It may take a little time, but it will come to her eventually."

"Thanks," he snarls as she removes herself from the room.

"Well, in a nutshell, Latavia, I am hurting like never before. Because of a misunderstanding, I ended up in the hospital, and you went off into the sunset and went half on a baby without me. Your father is dead along with your high school sweetheart, Nariah, my fucking boy B, and now Martinez. The baby is in NICU fighting for her life. I will be by her side because I vowed to love her as if she were my own.

"I'm not sure what act you may or may not be pulling not remembering anything, but right now I can't deal. I'm at my breaking point, so I am going to give you time to get yourself together. I will check in on you, but I really need time, Latavia. You hurt me to the core. By the way, we are homeless because of the incident with you and Mona's husband," he blurts out before leaving me in bed in tears, full of disbelief.

"Wait a minute! Wait a minute! How can you drop that load on me and then walk out on me? Nae's gone? Nard? And Martinez? Oh, my God, what have I done? Oh, my God! No, it can't be! Oh, my God!"

Nurse Lucas comes back. "Mrs. Carter, are you all right?"

"No, I am not. I can't stay here! I have to go fix things!"

"You are in no condition to leave, ma'am. Please try to calm down. We're going to give you something to help you relax."

Before I can protest, two more nurses enter the room, restrain me, and inject something into my IV. My eyes instantly become heavy.

Chapter Sixty-four

Granny Is Devastated

"Father God, please guide the hands of the doctors working on my grandbaby. Encamp angels around her and touch her from the top of her head to the bottom of her feet. I know she hasn't been in your will as she ought to be, but we all fall short of your glory, dear God. You said you will rain on the just as well as the unjust, and I come to your throne of grace on her behalf, asking you to rain your healing power on my Nikki. Father, she is nothing without you and needs your mercy right now, dear God. Let your will be done, not my will. I ask you all these things in your darling Son Jesus' name. Amen."

"Excuse me, Mrs. Neal?"

"Yes, sir, I'm Mrs. Neal. How's my grandbaby? Are you her doctor?"

"Yes, I'm Dr. Collins, and I have some bad news. We did everything we could possibly do . . . but Nicole didn't make it."

"Dear God! How?"

"Do you know if she had a history of hypertension or an existing aneurism?"

"Not that I know of. Are you sure there's nothing you can do for her? Please, Mr. Doctor, she's all I have left."

"I am truly sorry, but we did everything in our power to help her. She had a large amount of opiates in her system along with alcohol, which increased her blood pressure severely, causing her aneurism to erupt. Again, I am extremely sorry for your loss, Mrs. Neal."

"Jesus! Jesus! Jesus! Can I see her, Dr. Collins?"

"Yes, you can. I will have one of the nurses come out and get you."

"Mrs. Neal, how is she doing? I've been looking all over for you." Darnell approaches as Dr. Collins goes on his way.

"Not good, Darnell. My grandbaby's left me. I'm here all alone now. God, why didn't you take me instead? She was just a baby."

"Damn! Forgive my language, Mrs. Neal. I am so sorry. This day just can't get any worse. Why is God allowing this to happen?"

"Never question God, baby. It's in His will. We may not understand it, and the pain is unbearable, but He knows what He's doing."

"I think I'm beginning to have a hard time believing that. Too many people have been taken away from me at once. Maybe God doesn't love me."

"Hush now, you're talking foolish. He loves you. He has to because He is love. Sometimes we as people make decisions that get us into trouble, and therefore, we have to suffer the consequences. God gives us the choice, and it's up to us to make the right one, baby."

"I apologize. I guess I'm just hurting. You are an amazing woman, Mrs. Neal. Here you are, encouraging me through your own tears and pain. How selfish of me."

"Sometimes when we help others, we help ourselves in the interim. Why don't you go home and try to rest? Your wife and little girl need you, and you can't be there for them if you don't take care of yourself."

"Home? I don't have one of those right now. So right now, I'll have to rest in the waiting area until I figure something out."

"It's figured out. I have that big old house with no one but me and . . . Lord, have mercy. I have to tell Gabby about her papa. Father God, I need your strength."

"This is too much. I'll go with you to talk to her if you'd like. Are you sure it's okay for me to rest my head there? I can't go back to where we were staying."

"It's done. Please come with me to say goodbye to my grandbaby, and we can be on our way."

"Yes, ma'am."

Chapter Sixty-five

Darnell Reminisces

Being a police officer, I've viewed countless DOAs, but seeing Nicole's lifeless body lying there and not having something slick come out of her mouth kind of messed me up something bad. However, witnessing Mrs. Neal fall apart the way she did almost took me straight out of here. Damn, this shit is getting out of hand. Everyone around me has been taken away from me. Is this God's way of telling me I need to be alone? I don't know what the hell is going on. What I do know is I can't take too much more of it. I never imagined in a million years I would be laying my head under Mrs. Neal's roof or trying to comfort her. Shit, I never thought I'd see or talk to her again, quiet as it's kept. God surely does have one hell of a sense of humor.

One thing is for sure, I'm going to do whatever I can to be there for the baby and make sure to consistently visit with her. I just can't deal with Latavia right now. Deep down inside I love her with every ounce of me, but I can't help feeling like this is all her fault. I know she didn't physically kill anyone, but her actions had consequences and were the driving force for a lot of this shit to get started. Had she not fucked with Braxton, my boy would never have met that dizzy wife of his, and he'd still be here. I know I have to take responsibility for the part I played in not telling her about that shit with Nariah, but God in heaven knows I never expected to ever see, hear, or have any dealings with her again. Damn, maybe this was my fault. Had I been up front with her, she never would have run out of the house. This shit is all fucked up. I can't be upset with her. Both of us held secrets and are reaping the harvest of it.

"Darnell, get yourself together, and come on down for some dinner," Mrs. Neal summons from outside the bedroom door.

"Yes, ma'am," I reply, jumping out of bed. I haven't had an appetite in a minute, but whatever that woman is burning has my nostrils wide open. She was always a hell of a cook from the day I met her.

That was actually a comical day, thinking about it. It was my and Nicole's nineteenth date. I remember it because it was an odd number, but she'd said she was odd, and by the twentieth date, we would be damn near married, and her granny would never approve of her keeping me a secret. Nicole had a weird sense of humor, so I didn't think anything of it when she'd said that, but it was a sign. Shortly after meeting Mrs. Neal, Nicole pressured me to marry her with every ultimatum in the book. Mrs. Neal, on the other hand, was a little rough in the beginning, but she smoothed over in time. Maybe it was the result of Nicole springing me on her.

If I'm not mistaken, we had gone out for dinner and had just finished bumping uglies in the car. When we pulled up to this duplex home, I was caught a little off guard because I'd never been there before, and I knew it wasn't her place either.

Out of curiosity, I asked, "What? You bringing me to random people's homes to finish beating that kitty up?"

"No, silly, this is my granny's place. It's time for you two to meet. I told you before, by the twentieth date we would pretty much be married, and she won't like that."

"We can't just show up unannounced reeking of hot sex on a platter."

"It's been so long since Granny had some, she has no idea what fragrance sex is anymore. Her house is perfumed with the smell of the best Southern food, so no one—not even you—will smell sex in the air."

"If you say so."

"I know so. Now come on in. Granny, I want you to meet someone!" she screeched as she opened the door.

"Little girl, stop all that hollering. Now introduce me to your deep, dark friend."

"Granny!"

"Well, he is a special kind of black. Nothing wrong with it. I just didn't know they had them around anymore, that's all."

"Really, Granny?"

"Hush it on up, little girl, and take your friend into the restroom to freshen up while I make you two a plate."

"I apologize, Darnell. She doesn't mean any harm. She's just stuck in her ways."

"It's cool. It sure does smell hella good in here."

"Yeah. She cooks like she knows someone is going to stop by for something to eat. Just do me a favor and keep the cursing to a minimum. Granny is very religious and doesn't curse at all."

"That's cool. My mom was the same way. She didn't use profanity at all either. I don't know where I got it from."

"Probably from working with all them crooked cops."

"Watch your mouth."

When we got back downstairs, Mrs. Neal had the table draped with fried chicken, ham, turkey, macaroni and cheese, yams, greens, cornbread, potato salad, pies, and cakes. By reflex, I asked, "All of this on a Wednesday in the middle of summer? I think I'm in love."

"You can't be when you're smelling like my grandbaby's tail. Now sit down and eat."

It's still awkward thinking about that conversation, even over ten years later. But Mrs. Neal grew on me, and I grew on her over time, and she's a strong, nurturing, and loving old lady. She reminds me so much of my mom. That's why I've taken such a liking to her and why I am hesitant to be around her at the same time.

"Darnell? Boy, what are you doing over there? Come on in this kitchen, and stop acting like you're a guest in this house."

"Yes, ma'am. It's a little cold in here, Mrs. Neal."

"I have to turn the heater on. It's always colder in here than it is outside. I've been meaning to have the guys come and look at it for me."

"I can take a look for you if you'd like."

"I'd like you to come on in here and put some food in your stomach. I made your plate already, so go on and enjoy yourself."

"Mrs. Neal, when did you have time to make all of this? We haven't been here that long."

"I started yesterday and just had to reheat a few things, that's all. Now stop with all the questions, and eat your food, boy."

Mrs. Neal couldn't care less how old you are. She will call you boy and little girl without a second thought. I think this is what I need right about now to clear my mind and get some kind of structure in my life. I can't believe she made all of this food—the same spread she had on the day I met her. It looks like I've fallen in love with this lady all over again.

Tomorrow is a new day. I'm going to kick it with Granny and Gabriella for the night, and head on over to the hospital tomorrow morning to check on my wife and the baby. I think Mrs. Neal needs me right about now just as much as I need her.

Chapter Sixty-six

Latavia Remembers

I open my eyes to the realization that none of this is a dream. I am still hospitalized, and I've given birth to a baby I vaguely remember conceiving. Bits and pieces of everything flood my dreams, and the only things I recall are killing my father when I caught him with Nae and attending Nae's homegoing service. Those are the only things I seem to remember. It isn't adding up. I don't remember how Nae died. I can't believe she's gone. Walter deserved to die after what he did to me. I have no pity about whatever I did to him. Darnell just dropped a bomb on me and left me sitting here unable to breathe in complete shock. I have so many questions and no one to answer them.

"Latavia," a familiar voice sings from behind the door.

"Come in," I welcome her.

"How are you feeling, my friend?" Mona cries, kissing me all over my face.

"I don't know how or what to feel right now. I am alone and scared. The only things I remember are Nae's funeral and my father dying."

"You don't remember anything else at all?"

"No! Especially not all the things Darnell said before he left here angry because I don't remember anything."

"It will take time, but all of it will come back to you. Try to calm down. Wait, your stomach is gone! You had the baby already? Do you remember being pregnant?"

"No, and the last thing I want to be right now is someone's mother."

"Please don't say that. You're just upset. There are so many women who want children and can't have them. You're blessed to be able to bring a life into the world."

"Yeah, well, the way I feel, one of those women can have her because I can't do this right now."

"You're confused and upset. You don't mean that."

"I know what I'm feeling, and a mother isn't it."

"If you don't mind me asking, what did Darnell say to you that has you talking this crazy?"

"Nard, Martinez, Nae, and BK are dead. That baby is fighting for her life, and we are homeless because of an—"

"You don't remember any of that either?"

"None of it, Mona."

"Well, let's try to change the subject a little for now. Have you even seen your little girl yet?"

"Only the pictures from the nurses over there on the table, but honestly, I really don't want to see her."

"Maybe I should give you time to rest. I am going to see if I can check on your little girl," she coos as she drools over the pictures.

"That's fine, and you can take those pictures with you as well while you're—"

Before I can finish my sentence, she goes flying out the door. Oh, my God! It's all coming back to me. I am a horrible person! How can I face Mona or Darnell? Both of them love me dearly, and I've betrayed their trust in the worst way. I don't know what to do. I can't deal with any of it, especially not that little girl. She'll be a constant reminder of all my fuckups. No, thank you. If I keep up with not remembering anything, I think I can get over and past all of it. Hell, since Mona is so concerned about that plucked chicken–looking baby, she can have her.

Chapter Sixty-seven

Ramona Has A Revelation

I can't believe how selfish Latavia really is. This poor baby didn't ask to be here. It was her reckless behavior that brought this precious jewel into the world. I have to work my magic to convince the nurse that I'm Latavia's sister and, since she's still having some health issues, the child's father and I will be visiting. It works like a charm, and it isn't all a lie. Knowing what I've learned of Darnell, he will be everything he has to be for this child and his self-centered wife.

This little girl might be the vehicle to bring back the joy that was lost from my and Delvin's lives. I know he concealed his disappointment in me that I am unable to conceive, but it isn't my fault. I want to share with him what happened to me at the age of 16, but I am afraid. I have never told anyone other than my mom what happened to me. Although the memories of it haunt me day in and day out, I don't allow it to consume me—at least I try not to—but listening to my mom talk today brought back a lot of unresolved issues that I'd buried, in addition to shedding some light on some things I didn't know. We clearly have a raping generational curse shadowing my family from the sounds of things.

God knows it breaks my heart to have kept this from Delvin, but I don't want him to look at me differently because, in actuality, technically, I wasn't a virgin when we married. However, it wasn't by choice. My parents had spent so much time building the church house that they forgot to build a home. If they weren't vacationing somewhere, counseling a married couple, or at the church, period, Dad was in his private study, and Mom was locked in her room. This left me alone literally and emotionally.

On most school nights, I didn't have to attend the church services because my parents wanted to make sure I was alert in school. When I turned 16, I was allowed to stay home alone with no more babysitters to keep me company. Everyone in the church was considered family, so they dropped by unannounced and knew everything that went on in our house—like me being home alone—because we were all "family" if you let my parents tell it. Little did they know, not everyone in their congregation had their best interests at heart and considered us family, especially my dad's good and close friend Minister Evans.

Long story short, my dad's good friend had a serious problem keeping his hands to himself. For a month straight, he would come by and rape me over and over. He was angry and aggressive and hurt me physically and mentally. When he saw that I was beginning to gain weight, he put two and two together and stomped the baby out of me. I couldn't control the blood or stop the pain, so I told my mom everything. It broke her heart. However, she felt it would be best if we kept it from my dad, because she said he was dealing with so much at the time.

Mom made sure I was never home alone again or anywhere near Minister Evans, even though I had to see him in church and around the house all the time. It got to the point where I became immune to the pain, and seeing him didn't bother me anymore. That was until the conversation with my mom earlier and one other time when Latavia shared with me what she'd endured at the hands of her father as a child. We have so much in common, but I was too ashamed to share my pain with her, or anyone for that matter.

I just think with all that is happening and that has gone on, Latavia and Darnell need to continue staying with us so I can look after the baby. Latavia is in no condition to do so, and if need be, if it comes down to it, I can prove to the courts that she is unfit to care for the baby.

Either way, this is my baby. God sent her to Delvin and me, I think, holding on to my little girl's hand . . . I mean, the baby's tiny hand.

Oh, my God! My dad's friend my mom kept mentioning is Minister Evans. He is the only person my dad considers a "friend." That coward not only raped and beat me, but he is having a gay relationship with my father and is the reason my dad can't love my mom.

Chapter Sixty-eight

Delvin Needs A Break

I don't know Martinez like that, but I am a little shook up over his death. Life is way too short to be walking around unhappy and not living life to the fullest. I have been unhappy for quite some time, and I can't blame it on my wife because I'm responsible for my own happiness. Nariah made me happy. She was just so outspoken and down-to-earth that I couldn't get enough of her. Mona deserves more from me, and I can't give it to her right now. I am stuck on Nariah something awful, and these feelings for her won't let up. Maybe I need rehab or need to go away for a little while to give my marriage some space so I can regroup and get my head together.

Why can't I have a happy, normal marriage like my parents? They are so in love it's contagious, or so I thought. I used to pray that, when I got married, my union would mirror theirs. My pops never roamed or wandered away from Mom Dukes. If he did, he did a hell of a job keeping that shit on the low. When I told him I was thinking about marrying Mona, he was a happy, proud man with specific instructions, saying, "Son, you have a good woman. Make sure you keep those stray cats out of your yard and off your property. They pay little heed to fences and property lines."

"Now that's classic, Pops."

"Son, I'm serious. Some of them don't care that you have a collar around your neck, and they won't return you to your rightful owner. Instead, they will try to make you theirs."

"I hear you, Pops."

"I don't need you to hear me, son. I need you to listen to me. When you stray, you become a stray. Do you know what a stray dog is? It's a dog that's found in a place where it shouldn't be without its owner, not under the control of its owner or the person representing them."

"I don't need a woman trying to own me or have me under her control. I'm a grown-ass man."

"When you take ownership of something, you don't have to control it. You cherish, honor, love, and take care of it. That's your responsibility as a man and, most importantly, as a husband. Don't allow your generation to confuse you so you end up finding yourself in the category of a stray dog."

Damn, my pops had a point and had really schooled me, but evidently, I didn't learn shit. I am a fucking stray dog right about now, and a dangerous one now that I'm thinking about it. I've strayed to the point where I could be classified as a dangerous stray because I caused injury to Mona's heart, and she is now in fear of being hurt and injured again because of it. What can I do to fix this? Every time I look into her eyes, the guilt gnaws at me. I'm going to call her to see if we can sit down to talk things out. They say honesty is the best policy. Maybe if I am honest and upfront with her about everything, we can move on from here and start over. But what do I do with the feelings and memories of Nariah? No matter how much I confess and talk, I still have her engraved in my mind.

Chapter Sixty-nine

Darnell Makes Amends

I am amazed at how well I slept last night. Other than it being freezing in this place, it is so peaceful, considering we've both just lost someone dear to us. Sleep definitely allows me to operate on a clear and full mind. I am ready to tackle all that this day has for me. First thing I'll do is make sure Mrs. Neal and Gabriella are good. Then I'll make my way over to the hospital to see my wife and our little girl. It feels a little weird and surreal saying "our little girl," but that's who she is to the both of us, and I have to accept it.

The smell of breakfast seizes me, so I zip through my shower and get dressed in no time. The aroma has me running down the stairs as if someone is chasing me.

"No running in the house, Uncle Darnell. Granny's gonna get you," Gabriella snickers, meeting me at the bottom of the staircase.

"Shhhhh, don't tell her."

"I heard that. Now both of your sneaky tails get in here and get some of this food."

It's a sad shame Gabby's mom turned her back on her the way she did. Thank God she has Mrs. Neal . . . oh, and me. I'm trying not to think about Martinez, but it's hard not to. He was such a good person and almost like a brother to me. What the hell were he and Nicole doing?

"Good morning, Mrs. Neal. It sure smells good in here, and that spread looks even better than it smells."

"Why, thank you. Make sure you eat well so you have energy for your wife and baby girl."

"I plan on it, and thank you for allowing me to rest my head here. By the time Latavia is released from the hospital, I will have found a place for us, or we can just stay at the Marriott."

"Hush that foolishness. You and your wife and that baby girl are welcome here as long as you need it. No rush. I could use you guys here. I'm getting old, and I don't like being alone any longer."

"You aren't alone, Granny. You have me and my papa."

"Yes, I do, baby, but I need you to go sit at your table now. This is a grown-up conversation, princess."

"Yes, ma'am," she obeys, retreating to her table in the other room.

"As you can see, I haven't been able to break the news to her. It's a little hard for me to break that baby's heart again. I know there's no way I can keep it from her. I just need a little time. It's bad enough I have to try to deal with my own pain of losing my grandbaby."

"I completely understand. I think you should take all the time you need. It will be a while before the department is ready for his service. He has to have an autopsy, et cetera, and they need to make sure they look good in the public's eye."

"Why so?"

"They aren't sure what happened. They're saying it was a heart attack, but the captain told me otherwise."

"I knew something was going on with Marty. I saw it in his eyes. I was going to talk to him when he got back to pick up Gabby, but he never made it back," she said, tears flowing down her face.

Standing to hug her, I say to console her, "It will be rough for all of us, but we will get through it. You told me the other day God won't give us more than we can bear, so now it's time for us to stand on that promise, even through the pain."

"You're a great man, Darnell. Thank you. I needed that. Now get yourself back in your seat and finish your food."

"Yes, ma'am."

Mrs. Neal is a wonderful, strong woman with a purse full of pain she carries around. She tries not to open it up around people, but I can see right through her, and I recognize that same pain because I too can relate to it.

After breakfast, I head straight over to the hospital, excited to see my wife and to apologize, but she was taken for tests before I got here. The only question I have is, why am I nervous? I guess with all we've gone through and the way I left here yesterday, I'm feeling a little awkward.

"Look who decided to keep loving me," Latavia cries as they push her bed back into the room.

"I don't think it's possible for me to stop loving you, Latavia. Just because I'm upset doesn't mean I don't love you anymore."

"You were just so upset because I can't remember much. I'm sorry, but I keep trying to play back what you said to remember. Even when Mona came to see me, I tried to remember as we talked, but nothing is making sense to me. I just can't recollect anything, and I am so sorry, Darnell."

"It's all right. It isn't your fault. There's a medical reason why you can't remember, so there's no need to apologize. Right now, our main concern is getting you well and back on your feet so we can take care of our little girl."

"Our little girl?"

"The baby, Latavia. What do you want to name her? I was thinking we should name her after you and Nariah. What do you think about that?"

"That would be a jacked-up name, Darnell," she jokes. "But seriously, I'm not sure how I feel about any of this. I can't even remember giving birth or carrying a baby. I'm going to need some time to process all of this. I'm so sorry." She bursts into tears.

"Take all the time you need. I'm here for the both of you. We'll get through this together as a family."

"I'm the luckiest woman in the world to have you by my side."

"Don't you forget it either."

"How can I?" she replies, pulling my head closer to her as I reach down to kiss her soft lips.

"Wow, it's been a long time since we've done that. That was good."

"It will get better once I get out of here."

"Speaking of that, I'm not sure how you're going to feel, but we will be staying with Mrs. Neal until we find a place. She needs help with Martinez's daughter, and she's getting old. I thought it would be beneficial for all of us at this point."

"Darnell, who is Mrs. Neal?"

"This is going to be a little hard. If it becomes too much, stop me and we can talk about it later."

"I'm fine. Keep talking."

"Mrs. Neal is Nicole's grandmother. Nicole is my ex-fiancée. You sort of met her the day B's wife shot him. She is also your sister, and she passed away yesterday with Martinez."

"My sister? My mother didn't have any other children besides me."

"The day you got hurt and were rushed here, I ran into Nicole earlier that day. She dropped that bomb, telling me Walter was her father and she had just found out not too long ago."

"So you keep in contact with Nicole like that?"

"Like what? I just said I ran into her. What part of that didn't you get, and why is that the only thing that has your concern? You had a sister you knew nothing about, and now she's gone. That doesn't bother you?"

"It does. I'm just trying to process it all. This is all so much for me because I don't remember anything, and it's giving me a headache. Can we just hold each other? I just can't deal with too much more right now."

Sometimes I just don't get her. I understand that she's dealing with a lot right now, but to single out whether I keep in touch with someone out of all the things I shared with her is a bit much. Maybe I took it the wrong way, but that really struck a nerve.

Chapter Seventy

Latavia Dislikes Herself

I hope and pray Darnell hadn't lost his mind and wasn't out there messing around with her to try to get back at me. I made a mistake. I thought he and Nae were having an affair behind my back, so I wasn't all the way in the wrong. If he was out there screwing around, he was most definitely in the wrong, considering he'd said he forgave me and understood what happened between me and BK. All I know is we need to get through all of these mishaps in order to make our marriage work. I think it's time I go back to counseling. I refuse to lose Darnell because I allowed the ghost of Nae to take over my coochie. I am out of control and have to put a stop to it.

As for this Nicole person, how can she be my sister? My parents never once mentioned anything remotely close to that to me. Maybe it was a secret along with all the other secrets I've had to carry all my life. I hate Walter with everything in me. I'm sorry Nae had to take the fall for me and I didn't speak up for myself, but I was extremely upset with her at the time. To make things even more convenient, Nard had it all mapped out, and I just went with it. I mean, it literally got to a point where he'd made me believe I hadn't shot my father. Honestly,

I thought they would have gotten Nae off somehow, one way or the other. There's no way in hell I wanted anything to happen to her. All of this is entirely my fault, and now she's gone. I will always hate myself the more because of all this.

How can I fix the mess I single-handedly created? Let's not forget, I just so happened to have accused Mona's husband of raping me. Five will get you ten she knows all about it. However, me having this sudden case of amnesia helps defuse the situation and keeps her and the topic at bay. This needs to be fixed because it will all come back to haunt me, with my luck. Now I have this child I'm supposed to care for. How can I be a mother when I haven't mastered being an adult, friend, or wife yet?

"Latavia, what's on your mind? You're completely spaced-out over there," Darnell interrupts, pulling me away from my pity party.

"I'm fine. I just hate that all of this is a blur to me. Why can't I remember anything? It's driving me insane."

"Don't force it, Latavia. It will come in time. Right now, we need to focus on getting you in tip-top shape and healthy again. We have a little girl who needs both of us to be on our A game."

"I know, and that scares the hell out of me."

"How so?"

"I don't remember being pregnant or having her, and now I'm supposed to be a mother when I can barely remember who I am."

"Don't beat yourself up for not remembering. Dr. Givens said it will come in time and it's temporary. I believe if you keep stressing yourself to remember, it will make it worse."

"I'm trying not to, but it's hard not to at the same time. How am I supposed to be a loving mother to a baby I don't even know?"

"Just try to love her every day, and start over if you have moments when you beat yourself up about forgetting. I will tell you this—while you were pregnant with her, you were beyond happy and were in love with her as she grew inside you."

"With me not remembering, I can't get those memories or those feelings back. I can't even look at her, not feeling like she's mine."

"You won't know that until you try. How about we have the nurse take us downstairs so you can see her?"

"I really don't want to, Darnell."

"Latavia, I think it will help a lot. She needs you right now. That little girl is fighting for her life, and having us there could help her."

"How, if she doesn't even know we're there or who we are?"

"Stop talking like that. I'm going to get a nurse to see if we can take you downstairs. Just know that this isn't just about you, Latavia. It's about all of us."

I have to play this off no matter what. I just hope and pray I can when I see this damn baby.

"That was fast," I murmur as Darnell rushes back in the room with a wheelchair.

"This will be good for you, you'll see," he gloats as he assists me into the wheelchair.

"If you say so."

"Cheer up. It could be worse, Latavia."

"I know. I just don't know how to feel or what to expect."

Boarding me onto the elevator, he explains, "Those are normal feelings. I want to prepare you the way the nurse prepared me for what's going on and what you'll see in the NICU. That's the name of the unit babies are placed in when they are in intensive care. Because you delivered early, she won't look like a normal baby who was delivered at nine months. She is in an incubator, which is an enclosed crib, and she will have a lot of tubes in her. All of this is necessary to help our baby girl grow and breathe."

He is really trying to be a candidate for father of the year. This is all so wrong. She's really supposed to be our baby, I think as tears make their way down my face.

"I'm sorry. I didn't tell you those things to upset you. I just want you to know beforehand what's going on," he apologizes as we exit the elevator.

"It's okay. Let's go get this over with."

Chapter Seventy-one

Ramona Is On A Mission

I can't believe I'm still at the hospital. I tried to get the nurses to allow me to stay in the room with my princess, but that is frowned upon. They did offer me a nesting room where I am allowed to stay, which is a godsend because I just can't face or deal with Delvin. Deep down inside, I have a feeling something happened between him and Latavia, but I would hate to believe I'm married to a rapist. There is no telling what happened at this point. I've tried to erase it from my mind because I plan on doing whatever it takes to work on our marriage.

Then there's the other part of me that asks, *how can you work on anything when trust is absent from the equation?* Burying myself in Elite has run its course as I've hired staff and have everything running as if I were there. I need a distraction, and I believe this baby will be just that, along with giving me the happiness I long for. The only thing is convincing her mother and stepfather.

I think I'll go see the little princess before I go home to face the music and have a heart-to-heart with my husband. Who knew Latavia's child would bring me so much happiness? I know God has a way of working things out, and from listening to her the previous night, it sounds like she wants nothing to do with the child. Who would be a better guardian than me? Maybe I should talk with her first before I get my hopes up too high. Perhaps if she and Darnell continue to stay at my place, I'll be able to care for her as if she were my own until she becomes mine, just like I did with Elite.

Technically, I didn't do anything out of the norm other than work my ass off and give myself bonuses here and there, which I deserved. Latavia and Nariah allowed life to get the best of them and abandoned their company. I am the one who worked long hours to keep it afloat and bring in new business, so why wouldn't I compensate myself? If the Carters reconsider and stay with me, I know Latavia will push everything concerning the baby on me, and if she doesn't, I will volunteer my services. That way, when the time comes, I can prove she's unfit, and the State will award me custody. Darnell will be easy to bypass. He's the same man who lost his job, killed someone, and was placed in a psych ward. Looks like this will be easier than I thought.

Before I can finish my thoughts, my one-woman conversation, I am distracted by a familiar voice. "Mona, is that you?"

"Hey, Latavia. How are you feeling?"

"I guess all right. Everything is still a blur to me, but Darnell thought it would be a good idea for me to come see . . . Wait, what are you doing here?"

"I thought I'd come check in on you and your little girl. I visited with her last night for you."

"That's why I love you. You're always looking out."

"That's what friends are for, Latavia."

I guess she's getting her memory back if she remembers that. This can't be good for me. Either way, I'm going to do whatever I have to do to bring that little girl home with me.

"Well, I'll give you two some time and space to visit with your little girl. I have a few errands to run. I will come check in on you and the baby later, Latavia," I express, kneeling down to kiss her on the cheek.

"Thank you for everything, Mona. I appreciate you."

"You're welcome. Darnell, I apologize about the other day. Thank you for being honest with me."

"The other day? What happened the other day?"

"We had a disagreement about Delvin, but that's not important right now, Latavia."

"No problem, Mona. Can we talk about this another time?"

"Sure thing. I'll talk to you two later."

My mom said to trust the eyes, the eyes never lie, and I have a funny suspicion Latavia's memory loss isn't what she says it is. When she thanked me, she caught herself looking up at me like a deer caught in headlights. I will play her little game so I can get her to move back in before the baby is released from the hospital. The nursery she and I were going to set up at my place is still empty. I will set it up with the items we purchased together and show her pictures the next time I go to visit. Hopefully, that will butter her up to reconsider. Once she makes up her mind, Darnell will follow suit, which I do know from observation.

I have been so caught up in my thoughts I don't know how I got home so fast. Delvin's car isn't here. Good! I'm in a decorating mood, not a talking mood. Anxious and not paying attention, I throw my purse on the table, causing me to knock down an envelope addressed to me. It looks like Delvin's handwriting. *What in God's name does he have to say in writing that he can't tell me face-to-face?* I puzzle, opening the envelope. The note reads:

> *My Dearest Ramona,*
> *This is by far one of the hardest things I've ever had to do, but this is the only way for me to apologize and to tell you about how I have let you down and broken your trust. I'm not worthy of your love anymore. As you are aware, I have engaged in the sin of cheating on more than one occasion with two women other than Nariah, Latavia being one of them. I never meant to hurt you. Again, I am truly sorry. I can no longer live with myself, as my thoughts are consumed by Nariah. She is the only reason I slept with Latavia and the one other person who is the reason why I am on leave indefinitely from my job.*
>
> *The Delvin you married got lost in the shuffle when you took on one too many responsibilities at Elite and you neglected your primary responsibility: your husband. No, I'm not saying it's your fault this happened. I never imagined I would have fallen in love with Nariah, but I did, and because of this, I need to get some help so I can be the husband I used to be. Again, I am deeply sorry I couldn't face you to tell you this, but I needed to get it out. I couldn't bear looking into your brown eyes and hurt you all over again.*
>
> *You have been an amazing wife, and I have let you down. I am going away to try to find myself and get myself together so I can come back to*

you a changed man. I hope you can find it in your big heart to forgive me and, when I get back, we can work on us. I've never stopped loving you, Ramona. I'm just not in love with you, and I want back that old flame we had. I want to love you with everything in me, and again, I am truly sorry I've hurt you and betrayed your trust.

Above all, I know I have hurt you immensely, and I will never, ever do this again, I promise you that. But please give me a chance.

Love Always,

Your Ashamed and Apologetic Husband Delvin

Chapter Seventy-two

Granny's Heartaches

Lord, my heart is aching really bad. I need you to come on over here and touch this old ticker of mine. I can't allow anything to happen to me. These children need me. I know they need you more, but I'm the closest thing to you for them right now, so please touch my body. I need your healing hands on me now.

"Granny! Granny! Where's Papa? He hasn't come back yet."

"Come on over and let me talk to you, baby girl. You know I love you, don't you?"

"Yes, ma'am, and I love you more."

"You are so precious, and all I've ever wanted to do is protect you, but Granny can't stop everything, baby girl."

With a puzzled look on her face, she nods her head up and down, saying, "Yes, ma'am."

All right, Lord. Please give me the strength and the courage to break this baby's heart and put it back together.

"Gabby, your papa got sick, and the hospital couldn't help him. They tried to, but he was too sick for them to fix him, and he passed away. Baby girl, I am so sorry."

With tears streaming down her face, she sobs, "No, Granny. He can't die. I'm still a little girl. I didn't grow up yet. No, Granny, please bring him back. Please, Granny! Please!"

"The good Lord knows if I could, baby girl, he would be sitting right here with you. Just remember, your papa loved you, and God called him home to watch over you."

"No, Granny, I need him here to watch me, not up there," she weeps, pointing her finger upward.

"You have me, baby girl, and I promise not to leave you alone."

"Please don't ever leave me, Granny. I miss my papa! Can I go see him before he goes to heaven?"

"I will see what I can do, baby girl," I console her, hugging her and allowing her to cry on my chest.

This has to be the hardest thing an old lady like me has ever had to do. I think I need to go cook something to clear my mind after this baby finishes crying herself to sleep.

Staring up to heaven, I silently pray, *God, I know you know what you're doing, and I would never question you, but did you have to take both of those babies? Whatever it is you're doing, please don't do it without me. Please make it better for all of us, especially this baby. She done already had her momma walk out on her, and I'm all she has left. We all really need you like never before. Amen.*

Let me put some blankets on this baby. It sure is nippy in this house of mine. I will be sure to ask Darnell to bring up my old heating unit from the cellar when he gets in. In the meantime, I'm going to try to cook up something that will heat the place up and clear my mind. Cooking distracts me and helps me through the worst of times. Right now, my mind is all over the place. My Nikki is gone, and with her being stuck under that car, it done burnt up my grandbaby's beautiful face. There is no way I can allow an open viewing. These people won't be talking about my baby. It will be easier on me anyway if we keep it closed or have her cremated.

Falling back onto the bed, I whimper uncontrollably. I can't even move from here to the kitchen. The pain is bad. My heart is forever torn into little pieces.

Lord, is this your way of telling me to relax and deal with the pain? If it is, I need you to get me through this one. I can't do it alone.

Chapter Seventy-three

Delvin Seeks Help

When the affair with Nariah started, I really didn't know what I was thinking. I was kind of living in slow motion and never stopped to think about what was happening. I didn't allow my mind to go there most of the time. There were a few times on my way home from work when my hands were shaking so hard on the steering wheel that I was afraid I might have an accident. The guilt ate away at me day in and day out to the point where I couldn't even look my wife in the eye. I always felt sure she knew something was going on.

The bizarre thing in all of this was, although I felt guilty and ashamed, those feelings actually propelled me to continue the relationship and even start fucking around with Latavia—pregnant and all. It was like a release from anything going on in my life. I kept telling myself I was going to end things "very soon," but the release the sex provided made me feel alive. I can't explain it, but the more I think about it, the more I feel like a murderer because I killed what Mona and I had, all for a few nuts—literally.

Right now, I would give absolutely anything to turn back the clock and to take this whole thing back. Shit, if the roles were reversed and Mona did some shit like this to me, I would kill her ass dead. I am so wrong for what I've done. I can't even stand to look at myself any longer. To drive the nail in deeper, I chickened out and wrote her this bullshit letter and left it on the coffee table. There isn't a chance in hell I would have been able to look into her eyes and pour my heart out to her, being upfront and honest about everything. Break her heart even more? No, I can't do that. I am too ashamed and don't want her to look at me like this. A man is supposed to be strong and confident to his queen, and right now, I am neither. No matter what, I will keep trying to make it up to her for the rest of my life. If she will just give me a chance, I will do everything in my power to make things right.

My pops would be so disappointed in the man I've become. I've assumed the form of that stray dog he'd religiously tried to prevent me from turning into. I deviated from home and became a stray. Damn, isn't that strange? It was like Pops knew those stray cats would be all over my yard, at work, and at home. Ain't that about a bitch?

Apparently, I have a serious problem, because this shit cost me my job and my marriage. My livelihood has been stripped from under me because I can't keep my dick in my pants, when I have a beautiful wife at home. Something is severely wrong with me. I've been appointed a counselor by the job, and she recommended I go as an inpatient to The Center for Relationship and Sexual Recovery at The Ranch. The Center is located way the fuck in Tennessee, and they specialize in the treatment of serial infidelity along with a host of other things.

I figure this can help me keep my job and get my wife back. The woman at the Center I spoke with briefly said the therapy is to aid in disrupting and eliminating problems and patterns of sexual behavior while helping you regain dignity, self-respect, and the trust of those you love. That alone sold me on the treatment, because God in heaven knows a brother needs all the help he can get at this point.

I will be staying at the Piney Lodge, where I will detox before embarking on the process of my road to recovery. Never in a trillion years would I have imagined going to somebody's rehabilitation center, especially not over no damn pussy! But it is like Bell Biv DeVoe warned in their song "Poison" when they said never trust a big butt and a smile. Well, in my case, that head game was my poison downfall.

Either way, I'm headed to Tennessee to get the help I so desperately need in hopes of going back a changed man. I will write Mona a letter eventually to let her know where I am so she won't be worried.

"God, if you're up there, please protect my lady while I'm away, and please don't let any stray dogs end up in my yard."

Chapter Seventy-four

Darnell Is Annoyed

Damn, she's crying uncontrollably already. It pains me that I can't take the hurt and anguish from her. Sometimes I feel like less than a man when I can't fix things for my wife. I know I'm not God. I just want to protect her and make her happy at all times. Just my luck.

"Are you okay, Latavia? We can go back upstairs if need be."

"I think I'll be all right. How can I not remember being pregnant with her? Why don't I know her? She's supposed to be my flesh and blood, and I don't even know or remember her."

"Don't beat yourself up about it. It will come back to you. Just don't give up. I believe she needs you as much as you need her. You just don't know it yet."

"Honestly, Darnell, I don't think I'm mother material. I think I would ruin a child because I am so damaged."

"This isn't the place to talk about that. Let's just visit with her, and we can reconvene this discussion upstairs. Is that all right with you?"

"Yes, it's fine."

"This is probably the wrong time, but she needs a name. Did you think of one yet?"

"No, I didn't, Darnell. How can I think of a name for a child I don't even remember giving birth to? Can we go now?"

"Sure, that might be a good idea. The last thing she needs right now is negative energy around her."

"I agree. Why don't you ask Mona to continue visiting with her and to think of a name? I don't know what to call her, unless the name can wait until I get my memory back."

Escorting her to the elevator, I question, "What does Mona have to do with any of this?"

"One thing I do remember is Mona has worked for me for years and she knows me inside out. I'm sure she can think of the perfect name for me. She's good like that."

"It's strange you remember all the things about Mona but nothing about yourself. The entire calamity that happened in our lives is a mystery to you. The only things you recall are the good things?"

"Darnell, if I could make myself remember, I would. I have been trying to, but I can't. The last thing I recall is our wedding day, and that's it. Don't you think I am suffering to learn my sister and best friend is gone and I can't bring her back? I have been beating myself up since I found out. Maybe it would have been better for you and that baby if I'd never woken up," she sobs as the elevator doors open.

Hurriedly pushing her into the room, I comfort her through fresh tears of my own, saying, "Latavia, I'm so sorry I questioned your memory. This is hard on the both of us, and I was inconsiderate by not understanding how this is affecting you as well. Please don't ever question whether it would be better if you didn't exist. That would have destroyed me completely, so please refrain from talking like that. I love you with everything I am and everything I'm not. I need you and will be by your side through all of this."

"Thank you, Darnell. I apologize that all of this is happening, and I'm having a hard time calling to mind the past few months, or years for that matter, of our life. I will do my best to try to remember, I promise. Just know I love you and all I want is for you to be happy with me."

"Excuse me, Mr. and Mrs. Carter. I'm sorry to interrupt, but I have some great news. Mrs. Carter's test results came back, and everything looks great. It will be a process before she is one hundred percent back to herself, but she doesn't have to stay here through that process. We can release her and set up for a nurse to do in-home visits until she's in tip-top shape. She may also require some physical therapy for walking if it continues to be a strain for her."

"That's great news, Doc. What about her memory loss?"

"That should come back soon. The excitement over everything could be causing the memory lapse. Possibly when she gets out of here, everything could flood her mind and come right back to her. Like I mentioned earlier, she shows no signs of a concussion or anything else, so it should be just a matter of time before she regains her memory. I am going to prescribe you some pain medication and antibiotics to continue flushing you out, Mrs. Carter, and would like for you to follow up with your primary care provider."

"Great, thank you, Dr. Givens," we both sing in unison.

This is great news. I can take my wife home. Oh, shit, I need to make sure this is all right with Mrs. Neal. I know she said it isn't a problem, but now we will have a nurse coming in and out of her place also. She didn't sign up for that part of the deal. I will shoot her a quick call to make sure. If not, we will have to rent a hotel room or suite because there isn't a chance in hell we're going back to Mona's place.

"Latavia, give me a minute. I am going to step out of the room for a second to give Mrs. Neal a call to make sure everything is all right for us to stay there along with the nurse having to come back and forth. I am almost certain it won't be a problem. I just want to be sure."

"This should be interesting."

"What makes you say that?"

"We will be staying at your ex-fiancée's grandmother's home? That's a tad bit weird."

"I am going to ignore that. You always hang on to the wrong shit. We're homeless right now, and I wasn't engaged to or fucking Mrs. Neal, so what's the big deal? I'll be right back."

Sometimes this damn woman works my goddamn nerves in the worst way. Why the fuck is she worried about Mrs. Neal? Nicole isn't in the picture. She's dead, which I still haven't processed totally, but Latavia knows that I'm married to her. What is her issue, seriously?

Chapter Seventy-five

Mona's Master Plan

Sprawled out on the floor still in my clothes from yesterday, I lie there trying to comprehend what I just read. My husband has abandoned our marriage, saying he needs to get himself together and he's sorry for cheating on me not only with Nariah but with Latavia and some other female? How can this be? Am I that bad of a wife? Why on earth would he betray and disrespect me in such a manner? Especially in my home? I can't believe I opened my doors to be a friend, the only family Latavia had, and she turned around and gave me her ass to kiss right before spitting in my face. How could she do this to me and then, to take it a step further, disgrace my marriage by crying rape?

I trusted that wench around my husband without a second thought and in my home, and this is how she thanks me? Really? Hurt can't even begin to explain how I feel right about now. As for Delvin—the only man other than my dad I've ever loved—I don't know what I'm going to do with him. I'm most certain he was sincere and meant what he said because he didn't have to tell me anything, or did he? Is there something else he managed to omit from that so-called apologetic confessional? It's a good thing he didn't tell me face-to-face. I might have tried to kill him out of all the pain I'm carrying as well as all he has put me through. He's hurt me to my soul, and I don't think that type of grief is repairable.

This might very well be the anger talking, but I have a great gift of shutting people off and out of my life just like I've done with my dad. Right now, it looks like I will have to add my own husband to that blocked list. His going away can't and won't fix this or him. He's made his bed, so he'd best get real comfortable and lie in it, because I won't be there to keep him warm ever again. He's hurt me one too many times at this point. Enough is enough.

Now with reference to Latavia Carter, I am going to strip her of everything! She's never read any of the paperwork I had her sign for Elite. So with that, I am going to have my attorney draw up some paperwork turning Elite over to me, making me sole owner. I'm not sure what all needs to be done to make it happen, but I do know my attorney knows how to finagle things. The baby, on the other hand, might be my only battle. I wonder if I can have my lawyer draw up some additional paperwork saying she forfeited all of her parental rights, and since the child's biological father is deceased, she named me sole guardian. That might work. I know there will be a court date, which she will happen to miss, and the judge will have no reason not to award me custody. I'm brilliant. I just have to work my charm on my attorney.

In the meantime, I have to cover my anger up with a smile and try my best to treat Latavia the same so she really doesn't think twice about signing any of the paperwork once it's drawn up. My parents drilled the Bible into me, saying vengeance is the Lord's and He will fight our battles. I wholeheartedly agree. They also said you can catch more flies with honey than with vinegar, but the taste of revenge I have on my tongue tastes so much sweeter.

Chapter Seventy-six

Darnell Remains Quiet

Not for nothing, but I am a little nervous about bringing Latavia here. She feels some kind of way about being at Mrs. Neal's place. I know that woman has so much wisdom, and she will take my wife under her wing and help her get back to where she used to be, if not better. In any event, we're here now, so there's no turning back even if I wanted to.

"Mrs. Neal? Mrs. Neal? We're here. Is it all right for us to come in?"

"Sure thing, Darnell. I was resting. I'll be down in a minute," she shouts from upstairs.

"That's strange. She's usually cooking to feed an army, and the aroma seizes you as soon as you get in the door."

"Well, the only thing that greeted me at this door is a breeze. It is colder in here than it is outside. Oh, my God, Darnell," Latavia complains as I assist her inside.

"I apologize. I must have overslept trying to keep my mind right. All of this took me down a little, but I'm up now. You two come on in and make yourselves comfortable. I'm going to whip something together real quick for you and your beautiful missus."

"We don't want to put you out, Mrs. Neal. It's all right. We can order pizza or something. You need to take it easy just as much as we do. You're dealing with a lot, just like us."

"Hush your face, talking about ordering fast food. That stuff will kill you just as fast as you order it. Go on in there and get your wife situated while I put something on this stove. Oh, my Lord, forgive me, baby. I'm Granny. So nice to finally meet you, Latavia."

"Hello. It is my pleasure to meet you as well, Mrs. Neal."

"'Mrs. Neal' is so formal. Please call me Granny."

"I guess I don't know you well enough to be calling you Granny."

"Oh, I see you have a sassy one on your hands, Darnell! That must be your type, little boy."

"Little boy? Excuse me, Mrs. Neal, but my husband is a grown man."

"Latavia, chill out. It's all right."

"It's all right, Darnell. She'll learn me real good, I promise you that one. Now back to you, little girl. Mind your manners when you're speaking to me. I don't care how old or grown you may think you are. You might not know me, as you said, but you're about to know this backhand I've been blessed with when I knock your teeth down your throat. Now watch your mouth."

"Darnell, I don't know who this lady thinks she's talking to like that, but I'm not the one. She doesn't know me like that."

"Latavia!"

"You don't even know who you are! That's why you done messed over this good man God so graciously blessed you with. I hear things, and I know you haven't done right by this man, but I don't blame you. I blame him. He always falls for your type, and it jams him up every time. He loves so hard that he can't see the truth for what it is, even when it's sitting on his lap."

Right now, I'm going to remain quiet because Mrs. Neal is going to lay into my wife until she gracefully bows out. Little does Latavia know, she's fighting a losing battle.

"He has a type and he's jammed up? You have no idea what you're talking about, old lady. Look, I appreciate you extending your hospitality by letting us stay here, but if you want respect, you have to give it."

"Little girl, the one thing you lack the most, which is the most important thing you need to obtain, is respect. Don't come in here throwing around words you struggle with. I know you done messed over this man real bad, but I'm here to set you straight so you don't end up all by yourself. That's why God had me call Darnell and then run into him at that hospital. It wasn't a coincidence. It was divinely orchestrated because your ill-mannered tail needs some correction, and I'm here to give you just that. Now go on in that living room and get comfortable while I put some food together for your disrespectful behind," she reprimands her before excusing herself to the kitchen.

Rolling her eyes and shaking her head, Latavia mumbles, "I am a grown woman. No one will talk to me like that."

"Latavia, baby, please calm down. Mrs. Neal doesn't mean any harm. She calls everyone she loves little boy and little girl. It's like a term of endearment."

"She doesn't even know me to love me, and she is a little disrespectful. I am a grown woman. No one will talk to me any kind of way. I'm not having that!"

"I really think you should listen a little to her. She isn't trying to hurt you or us. All she wants to do is help us.

The way I see it, we can use all the help we can get."

"The only person around here that requires help is her old ass."

"Look, Latavia, I'm not taking sides, but she isn't Nicole, Nariah, or some girl in the streets. Mrs. Neal is a woman with years of experience and a boatload of wisdom. We can learn so much from her if we listen and not fight against it. I'm not saying she knows everything, but I do know experience is one of the wisest teachers. The things she says might come out wrong at times, but if you pay attention, you'll catch on to the intended message. Just take the meat and throw away the bones."

"I guess I just don't like her delivery."

"That's because you came in here in a defensive stance, so no matter what she said or didn't say, you were going to take it to heart."

"Maybe you're right. I'll fall back and not be so defensive. I guess all of this is getting the best of me. I just feel like I don't know anyone, and everything around me is caving in on me. I am so sorry, Darnell."

"I'm not the only one who deserves an apology."

"You have a point."

"I understand, my love. I know all of this is a lot for you and won't help bring your memory back. Just try to listen to some of the things Mrs. Neal says, opposed to just hearing her. My first encounter with her wasn't pleasant either, but she grew on me. Trust me, listening to her will do you more good than harm in many ways. I'm not saying this because she gave us a place to rest our heads either. Mrs. Neal is a strong woman with an enormous amount of wisdom that both of us could stand to feed off."

"Darnell," Mrs. Neal summons me from the kitchen.

"Yes, ma'am?"

"Can you do me a favor and go on down to the cellar and bring that heater up for me? It's a bit cold in here, and your wife doesn't need a cold or anything else trying to attack her body while it's trying to heal. We need to get her better for your little girl."

"Yes, ma'am."

That lady is truly a godsend. I just have a feeling we're in the right place at the right time so Latavia and I can bury the past in order to embrace whatever the future has in store for us. I don't know what it is, but I have a strange feeling that being here will bring us close to or right at the door of our destiny. Just hearing her views and receiving her correction will go a long way for the both of us.

Chapter Seventy-seven

Granny's Discernment

I can't believe I overslept. That is a clear sign my mind is troubled. That's also God's way of telling me I need rest in order to deal with this bitter, hurt, and wounded little girl Darnell brought in here.

"Lord, I didn't put anything in these pots for these babies. There are a few leftovers in the fridge. I'm sure I can whip something up. Gabby done cried her poor self to sleep on a semi-empty belly. I don't want to wake her. She's had a rough day. I'll just put some supper to the side in case her tummy starts calling her in the middle of the night."

"Mrs. Neal, where would you like me to put this thing?"

"You can plug it up at the top of the stairs so it can take the chill off up there. This oven can take care of us while we're down here."

"No problem."

"Thank you, baby. Dinner should be ready in five minutes. I put some leftovers together. Have your wife come on in the dining room and get settled at the table."

"Yes, ma'am."

Now that the table is set, let me go on and have a seat. I don't have much of an appetite, but I will join these babies at the table.

"Darnell, do you mind blessing the table?"

"Not at all. Dear Heavenly Father, we want to thank you for this spread that Mrs. Neal—I mean, Granny—calls leftovers. Bless the hands that prepared this feast so she will be able to continue to be a blessing to our stomachs. Amen."

"Little boy, you'd better stop playing with the Lord when you pray."

"Mrs. . . . Granny, with all due respect, me and the Lord are cool like that. I wouldn't be able to talk to Him if I couldn't be myself."

"Well, you have a point. Now dig in."

"Don't mind if I do. I'd hate to see what you would have prepared had you not had any leftovers. We have greens, ham, macaroni and cheese, potato salad, cornbread, and yams. Lord, is it Thanksgiving in October?"

"You're so silly, little boy. Latavia, are you all right over there? You're mighty quiet, baby."

"Yes, I'm fine. I want to apologize for earlier. I'm dealing with a lot, and I didn't mean to take my frustrations out on you."

"It's all right. As long as you recognize the problem, that's half the battle. Now try to get some food in you so you can regain your strength and energy for yourself and your little girl."

"Thanks. I'll try."

"You don't sound sure of yourself. Is there something else bothering you?"

"I'll be all right."

"Just talk, Latavia. It might help," Darnell interjects.

"Well, Mrs. Neal—I mean, Granny—since I came out of the coma in the hospital, I haven't been able to remember anything. The only thing I recall is marrying my Darnell. I don't recall being pregnant, my friend passing, or anything else that's happened."

"I'm sure when you saw your little one, everything came to you, right?"

"No, and I didn't feel anything."

"It sounds like you have a case of selective memory loss, unless the doctor called it something else."

"I don't have selective memory loss. If I could remember, I would."

"Maybe it's time you went and saw a doctor to help you with all the trouble you're dealing with on the inside. You remind me so much of my grandbaby. I can see why he fell for you. The both of you are the same. Your daddy done passed down some troubling demons to you and your sister that only God and a doctor can cure."

"My daddy didn't pass down anything except mental, physical, and verbal abuse."

"I thought you didn't remember all of that, baby?"

"How can I ever forget the things he did to me? I don't think that type of stuff can just vanish from your memory."

"That's the same hold that baby has on you no matter how much you sit here and tell me you don't remember her. You know her just as much as she knows you. You don't want to face something, but I see right through you."

"You know what, Mrs. Neal or Granny, whoever you are? You don't know anything, and I'm not going to sit here and allow you to make me feel like I've done something wrong when I haven't."

"Little girl, you done did that all by yourself. You know you've done something wrong. Now sit your tail back down and eat your food. You can barely walk, so save the dramatics, acting like you're about to walk yourself away from this table. Listen here, I'm not here to make you feel anything you don't already feel. The truth hurts, and it will hurt even more if you hide from it. What you need to do is think about everything you're hiding from and deal with it because, if you don't, it will deal with you, and I'm sure you won't like the outcome.

"You have a good man right here. He isn't perfect, but he's perfect for you. Talk to him and stop your foolishness, playing the victim. Something is either hindering you from remembering because you don't want to face reality, so part of your past is blocked out, or you're intentionally blocking it out. Whatever it is, you need to deal with it, baby. You're too old to be walking around with all this drama. Life is too short. That little girl upstairs lost her papa, her momma done walked away from her, and now she has no one but me, who's almost a stranger to her. Do you want your baby girl to feel that same void and abandonment?"

With tears cascading down her face, she murmurs, "No, I don't want anyone to suffer the way I've suffered. I'm so sorry."

"I'm not the one you need to apologize to. It's that man sitting next to you. No, I don't know everything that's going on in that head of yours, but your eyes tell me it isn't good, and there's more to all of this than you've let on. If you need a moment, take one, take two, but get this man out of the dark no matter what price you have to pay. You owe him that much."

With her head bowed as if she is praying, she asks, "Can we be excused? Darnell, I think it's time we had a talk."

"Sure thing. I'll just wrap this food up. It will be in the microwave if you get hungry later."

Chapter Seventy-eight

Darnell Learns The Truth

I don't know what I just stepped into, but my gut is telling me to brace myself because I'm about to get sucker punched. Latavia is in the shower. Granny has one of those chairs in the bathroom so she can sit down and wash herself. After cleaning it off, I helped my wife in and allowed her to try to wash her troubles away.

"Hey, God, it's your boy D. I need a favor. Please give me the strength, patience, and understanding to hear my wife out. Thanks, God. Amen."

I think Latavia is finally going to come clean about killing her pops. That has to be what's eating away at her, because she never confessed or mentioned it to me. I was thinking it was something worse. What, I don't know. I'm ready for this conversation. Whew, that makes me feel better, considering I already know.

"Hey, Latavia, are you all right in there? Are you ready to come out?"

"Yes. I can't hide in here forever."

Noticing the stream of fresh tears pouring from her eyes, I nervously ask as I help her out of the bathtub, "Am I hurting you? Are you in pain?"

"No, but I've hurt you, and I'm about to put you through more pain, and it's tearing me to pieces."

"I believe I can handle it. Try me."

"I heard and listened to everything that old lady said. It's like she has some special powers or something and can see right through me. That scares me to death."

"She just has a way with words. Mrs. Neal is a very spiritually wise woman. She just picks up on things. It's like her calling or something."

"Well, she called me right on out, and I have to be honest with you about everything. This is really hard for me, but I've caused enough damage. Can you get me a glass of water while I put on some clothes Mrs. Neal left in here for me? I am assuming they belonged to her granddaughter. Also, I need to text Mona to let her know I was released from the hospital and to give her the address of where we're staying so she knows where I am."

"Yes, and you have nothing to be afraid of either. By the way, there's an envelope addressed to Mrs. Neal on the nightstand with the address on it."

"Thank you."

Taking two steps at a time, I hurry down, grab a glass of water, and take three steps at a time to get back into the room in record time. She appears to be still texting Mona. I'm in a pretty good mood because this is going to work out. I already know what she's about to say, but I'll let her tell me her way. It might make it easier for her to get herself together and not carry all the pain she carries around all the time.

"Here you go, baby," I say and hand her the glass of water.

"Thank you," she mumbles before taking the water down in one gulp.

"Would you like some more?"

"No, thank you. I want you to know I love you. I hope after I share everything with you that we can pick up what's left of us and make it work. All I ask is that you let me speak before you say anything so I can get it all out, if that's okay with you?"

"It is fine, Latavia, and we will work through whatever it is, I promise."

"For the record, I had no idea you and Nae had a one-night stand before I ran off with BK. I'm sorry I didn't ask questions or stick around. Running and hiding is what I do best apparently. Anyway, this is so hard for me, but after Nard came to get me from Connecticut, BK started acting funny, so I followed him to the hotel. When I got there, Nae was checking in, so I waited a minute before going upstairs, assuming she was there with BK. However, when I got to the room, Walter, my father, came out of the bathroom. I lost it and shot him."

"I know, Latavia, but why?"

"Darnell, please let me finish."

"I apologize. Continue."

"I passed out after it happened as you know, and while I was in the hospital after Nae pulled the gun on me, Nard visited me and said she'd shot Walter, not me. He was so convincing that, at one point, I thought maybe I hadn't, so I went with it, but deep down inside, I knew the real truth."

"Are you finished?"

"No, there's more."

Chapter Seventy-nine

Latavia's Confession

Confession is always weakness.

I guess it's now or never. I have a hole in the bottom of my stomach. I'm so afraid to tell Darnell all of this, but I feel like if I don't, Mrs. Neal will. She might not know all the details, but her intuition will snatch it out of me. It's now or never. I've already opened the door. I might as well finish walking through it.

"Please remember, no matter what I've done, I never once stopped loving you, Darnell."

"I love you more, Latavia. Now what is it?

"I wasn't truthful before my accident in the bathroom. Delvin didn't rape me."

"So what happened?"

"Please just let me finish before you speak, Darnell. This is really hard for me, but I don't want any more secrets between us."

"What happened, Latavia?"

"I . . . I agreed to have sex with him. He didn't rape me. I only said that because I was afraid and ashamed."

"What the fuck do you mean, you agreed to have sex with him?"

"Please lower your voice. I don't want Mrs. Neal to hear us."

"Mrs. Neal is the least of your problems. Now answer the damn question. What the fuck do you mean, you agreed?'

"I really don't know why or how. It just happened."

"So you're telling me you slipped and your pregnant pussy just happened to land on his dick? Do I look fucking dumb to you, Latavia?"

"No, you don't, Darnell. Why are you talking to me like that?"

"How the fuck else am I supposed to talk to you, Latavia? Honestly, did you think I would be able to just brush this under the rug? Not only were you pregnant by another man, but now you're sitting here straight-faced, telling me that you, while pregnant, had sex with your employee's husband? The husband of the same woman who extended her home to you? Ramona, the same woman who runs your fucking company as if it were hers, Latavia? Is that what you're telling me?"

"It's not like that, Darnell. I don't know what happened. It was like I had an out-of-body experience when I walked in on him masturbating. We weren't having sex, but then it was like something came over me, and we had sex. I am so sorry, Darnell. I didn't mean to do it. I really wish I hadn't either. He was very rude and mean, talking about he'd only had sex with me because I reminded him of Nae—"

Not allowing me to finish my sentence, Darnell smacks me across the face, knocking saliva out of my mouth.

"Shit, Latavia, see what you made me do? I am so sorry I lost my cool. I never should have done that to you. I am so sorry. You just fucked me up real bad. I think I need some air. I have to get away from you."

"Darnell, please don't go! We need to talk this through. Just promise not to put your hands on me again."

"I'm not going to hit you. I'm just unsure how much more I can take before I snap the fuck out."

"There isn't anything else, other than I do remember everything, and I remember and know our baby. That's all of it, and I am so sorry. I really love you, and I want to make us work."

With a lone tear flowing from his right eye, he grieves, saying, "Latavia, the only person you love is you. There's no way in hell you love me or anyone else. Love would have kept your legs closed no matter how long it had been since we'd had intercourse. Love would have listened instead of running off with another man. Love damn sure wouldn't have abandoned her premature baby in the hospital. I fought for you. I fought for us. I forgave you and trusted it was a mistake, only to get smacked in the face with you sleeping with Mona's husband while pregnant with your high school sweetheart's baby. That's some fucked-up shit, Latavia!"

"Don't you think I feel horrible about it? I'd have rather died than to have told you these things. The last thing I ever want to do is hurt you, Darnell."

"It's the last thing, but the one and only main thing you've been consistent with, and you keep doing it over and over again."

"Do you think you can find it in your heart to forgive me one day?"

"That's a really good question. You've hurt me beyond repair, Latavia. No one has ever hurt me more than you have, over and over again. All I've ever done is love you unconditionally with everything I had, even when I didn't think I knew how to at times. When you were dealing with things, I found a way to love you. Listening to you, I wonder what it was about you that I actually loved, because clearly I don't know you. You are not the woman I married or thought I was marrying. I really don't know what to do at this point or how to feel. This type of pain is so powerful, I honestly don't know if it is repairable. I know they say hurt people hurt people, but I think you've damn near killed me and all the love I had. It's getting late, and I am tired all of a sudden. We can talk about this tomorrow. In the meantime, I'm going to sleep in the chair over here. You can have the bed. Good night."

Through a tsunami of tears, I reply, "Good night, and I do love you. You showed me what it feels like to be loved. The sad part about it is that the feeling was so unfamiliar that I ran from it, and I'm sorry."

Chapter Eighty

Ramona Is Dumbfounded

I've managed to pull myself together and head on over to Leibowitz & Leibowitz to consult with my attorney and childhood friend, Cindy Leibowitz. Cindy is an African American woman with a Jewish last name because her adoptive parents wanted her to feel like she was theirs no matter who'd carried her for nine months and pushed her out. Larry and Diane Leibowitz were barren and couldn't have children of their own, which led them to Wings of Hope Adoption Agency. On their very first visit, they fell in love with 3-month-old Cindy Watkins.

Cindy's mom had given her up after coming home from the hospital to find that her fiancé of two years had packed up his belongings and most of hers and moved out without a forwarding address. Norma, Cindy's biological mother, didn't want to repeat history and be like every other woman in her family and wear the title of single mother, so she did the best thing for Cindy and put her up for adoption.

The amazing thing about Larry and Diane was they didn't want Cindy to grow up or be raised in the dark, so they did the necessary research and background checks to find Cindy's biological parents and were able to contact Norma. Norma agreed to meet Cindy when she was 16 years of age, and that was when she'd apologized to Cindy, giving her the details and reasoning for not raising her herself. It was also around the same time she and I met. Cindy was heartbroken, so she did what most of us do when we have no other person or place to turn to: she ran to a house of God, which happened to be my dad's church. She and I hit it off from our very first encounter.

I've never shared what was going on in my personal life with Cindy other than the good things, so it will be a surprise to her when I disclose what I want to do to Latavia, who she knows to be the best boss and so-called friend one could ever have. Hell, Cindy will realize she's been fooled just like I have been all this time. That woman really pulled the wool over my eyes.

Now that I'm thinking about her, Cindy used to ask me how much I really knew about Latavia, and if I thought I should allow myself to build a personal relationship with my boss, because mixing business with pleasure doesn't always work. I assumed Cindy was jealous of my loyalty to Latavia because Cindy and I were good friends, but I retained her as my personal attorney as well as the business attorney for Elite. Maybe God was using her to warn me and open up my eyes, but of course, I ignored her and didn't heed the warning.

Entering the stylish yet extremely classy offices of Leibowitz & Leibowitz, I greet the receptionist, saying, "Good morning, Phyllis. Did Cindy get in yet?"

"Good morning, Mrs. Michaels. She's running a little late but will be in shortly. You can wait in her office if you'd like."

Just hearing her acknowledge me as Mrs. Michaels makes my stomach turn. "Thank you, Phyllis. I will help myself to some coffee and wait for her."

"No prob. Speaking of her, she's coming through the door now."

"How are you doing, counselor?" I greet her as she enters.

"You're so silly. To what do I owe this honor and privilege this early in the morning for you to grace me with your presence? Did I forget it was my birthday again?"

"Look who woke up with a bagful of jokes this morning."

"Seriously, it isn't like you to pop up unannounced. Is everything all right?"

"Can we get into that in your office?"

"Sure thing. You can follow my lead in those cute shoes."

"Thank you. I clean up nicely after what I just went through," I confide in her as we enter her office.

"Have a seat. What's going on, and before you begin, is this on or off the record?"

"Honestly, that's up to you."

"This must be serious. Please continue."

"Well, long story short, Delvin had a few affairs, one of which I found out about at my boss Nariah's funeral. He had never once mentioned he knew her, and because of her free-spirited lifestyle, I made sure to keep my marriage and husband as far away from her as I could. Anyway, at the service, he lost it and fell to his knees, weeping over her."

With her eyes about to jump out of her head, she says, "I am so sorry. That's awful."

"I was mortified. He later confessed that, while she was locked up, he had an affair with her, and I forgave him. Silly of me, because once a cheater, always a cheater."

"That's not always true. We all mess up sometimes, and when we realize what we've done, it opens our eyes."

"His eyes must be stitched shut, because he also had an affair with Latavia in my home."

"Excuse me? Isn't she pregnant? Didn't I tell you to be careful moving that woman and her baggage into your home? I told you, if you let anyone move in, it should have been her husband, because he appears to be the only civilized one."

"You were right. I thought you were just saying those things because you were against me having a close bond with someone other than you."

"We aren't in high school, Ramona. You have other friends just like I do. I said that to you because, although you'd never disclosed to me how Latavia got pregnant or too much about her other than who her husband was and that she was your boss, I already knew all of those intricate details of her life."

"You did a background check on her? But why, if you weren't jealous of our friendship, Cindy?"

"I had my reasons."

"What, when you know nothing about her other than what I've shared with you and you don't know her from a can of paint?"

"I never communicated this with you, however, I wanted to know more about who you were doing business with and what you may or may not have been getting yourself into. So I did an extensive background check on Latavia. In my findings, I found out my father was murdered."

"I'm so sorry to hear that, but what does that have to do with anything?"

"I had a private investigator look her up, and he found out everything about her, including that her unborn child isn't her husband's."

"This shit is getting out of hand. To say this is a small world is an understatement. It is completely insane."

"Since when did you start cussing?"

"I think just now. This is unbelievable."

"I'm sorry I never told you, but I didn't want it to infringe on our sisterhood."

"The only thing that could or would infringe on our friendship is if you slept with my husband, mother, or father."

"Well, that's the least of your worries. You know I don't get down like that."

"Wow, I'm at a loss for words."

"I know you are. Did you come here to tell me about the affairs only?"

"No, I want to take Elite from Latavia and take that baby from her. She deserves to suffer the same pain she inflicts on everyone around her."

"Ramona Michaels, what in the world has come over you? I have never heard you speak in this manner."

"Hurt, anger, and betrayal have made their presence known and have taken over. I want that evil woman to pay for her infidelities, and I want her to suffer dearly."

"You're scaring me, Ramona! Think about what you're saying. You can't just take her company unless you do it illegally. She doesn't even have you listed as an owner or member of the company. To even try to buy her out or anything, you'd need her to add you as either a part owner or a member and include every intricate detail in the LLC operating agreement."

"Member? Explain that part please."

"A member is a part owner. They mean pretty much the same thing."

"Considering I pretty much run the company and Nariah is gone, I'm almost certain we can make that happen."

"If you can make that happen, I will do everything in my power to make sure Elite is handed over to you."

"You would do that to your 'sister'?"

"For starters, the only real sister I have is sitting in front of me with tears streaming from her eyes. Second, I hate cheaters and backstabbers. Blood doesn't make you family. Loyalty does."

"You're right about that. What about the baby?"

"Do you think you can get her to grant you temporary custody?"

"Yes, without question."

"Really? You sound very confident that it won't be a problem."

"The last time she and I spoke, she didn't remember being pregnant and pretty much wanted nothing to do with the baby."

"I can have Phyllis draw up the paperwork right now outlining everything. If she doesn't remember, maybe she'd willingly sign. From what you've just said about her not wanting anything to do with the baby, getting permanent custody of the baby may not be much of a hassle after all."

"Phyllis draws up paperwork? Isn't she the reception-ist?"

"She wears many hats. I had to let my paralegal Tamaria go. She was sleeping with all the men in this place, and their wives kept showing up trying to beat her into another dimension."

"I see there's a lot of that going around," I reply, shaking my head.

"You have no idea, and I am so sorry Delvin and that heffa did this to you."

"It's fine. Speaking of the heffa, she was recently released from the hospital and gave me the address where she's staying. I'm going to go pay her a nice little visit when I leave here."

"Ramona, in order for this to play out as planned, you have to put back on that good-girl charm and act as normal as you possibly can, as if nothing has happened or as if you're still in the dark."

"I'll do my best."

Chapter Eighty-one

Ramona Is Devastated

Of all the people in the world, Cindy just so happens to be sisters with Latavia. If that isn't the craziest thing in the world, I don't know what is. Yes, I do—my parents never had sex, and I'm a test-tube baby. God, you must have something extremely great in store for me, because all of this is a little much. I have literally been on the longest emotional roller-coaster ride called life. Every time I get off, I am thrust right back on. What have I done to deserve all of this broken and devastated excitement?

I've put on my good-girl face, as Cindy calls it, and I'm heading over to the Flushing Avenue address Latavia texted me. I tried calling her to let her know I was stopping by, but she never picked up. She's probably asleep. I am about to be her alarm clock, because I'm here, and I'm waking her and everyone else up.

Stepping outside the car, I can hear alarms going off, and the closer I get to the door, the louder they are. It sounds like the smoke detectors or something. Banging on the door as loud as I can, my attempts go unheard. No one's answering. I don't smell smoke or see anything. Their car is out here, so I know they're inside. I check the doorknob to see if it's open, but it isn't. Grabbing my phone, I hurriedly call 911, screaming into the phone, "Please come to 6798 Flushing Avenue. The smoke detectors are going off in the home where my friend is staying, and no one's answering the door. Please send someone!"

Before she can respond or I can hang up the call, I hear sirens. Thank God!

Running to the police car, I frantically spit, "I've been banging on the door, and no one's answering. Do you hear the smoke detectors going off? Oh, my God, please help them!"

"Ma'am, please try to calm down. Are you sure someone's in there?"

"Yes, their car is right there! Why aren't you trying to break the door down to get inside?"

"I need you to go stand across the street. Those are the carbon monoxide alarms ringing. The FD is en route."

"What the hell is FD? Carbon monoxide alarms? Oh, my God, no!"

Everything is a complete blur now. I see the firemen and police officers running in and out of the house. Their mouths are moving, but I can't comprehend what anyone's saying. I think I'm about to pass out.

"Ma'am, are you going to be—" is the last thing I hear before passing out. I wake up in an ambulance to learn that Latavia, Darnell, a woman named Mrs. Neal, and a 6-year-old little girl have been pronounced dead.

"This can't be happening, Officer. Are you sure they're all dead?"

"Yes, ma'am. I'm truly sorry for your loss."

"I can't breathe. I need to get out of here. Please let me go. I can't sit here."

Running out of the back of the ambulance, I reach for my cell phone, which just so happens to ring as soon as I touch it. Answering on the first ring, I cry into the phone, "Delvin, Latavia and Darnell are dead. I was upset, and I wanted her to pay and suffer for betraying me, but I never wished death on her."

"Mona, did you—"

"No, I came to the house too late, and they're gone. I can't believe this."

"Calm down. I'm going to come back home now. I was calling to tell you where I am, but I'll be there in three to four hours. I love you and I'm sorry."

Snotting into the receiver, I babble, "I love you too."

Not knowing where to go or what to do, I jump in the car and drive straight to the nursing home. I need my mother right now. All of this is too much. I'm in so much pain right now. What about the baby? She really doesn't have a mother right now. Who were Mrs. Neal and the 6-year-old little girl? Lord, why did they all have to go? The more I think, the harder I press on the gas, arriving at the nursing home in record time.

Bolting through the doors, I run straight into my mother's room to find her and my father talking. I fall to the floor at their feet. "I am so sorry for everything. Life is too short, and tomorrow is not promised. I don't want to be mad any longer. I can't lose the two of you. I am sorry. Please forgive me for being angry," I weep.

"Ramona, we love you and it's all right. Please try to relax. We aren't going anyplace anytime soon, princess," my father consoles me.

"Dad, you don't understand. I was angry with Latavia, and I was planning evil against her. When I went to confront her and put my plan into motion, the carbon monoxide detectors were going off. She, her husband, and two other people—one a little girl—were pronounced dead."

"Jesus!" Mom blurts out.

Hugging me with all his might, my dad consoles me, "You didn't kill her, princess. I know you were angry with her, but it isn't your fault. You can't beat yourself up or blame yourself. It is a tragedy, undoubtedly, but it isn't your fault."

"He's right. It isn't your fault," Cindy confirms as she enters the room.

"It sure feels like it is. I was so hurt. I just wanted her to feel the same hurt she'd put me through, and now she's gone."

"After you left, I had a bad feeling about you going over there. I didn't want you to blow up on her, so I jumped in my car, not knowing exactly where I was going. I lost sight of you, but when I heard the sirens, something told me to follow the sound, and I arrived as you sped off. After speaking with the detectives, I was informed that apparently an old propane heater was brought inside to heat the home, and it had stopped working. The coroner's office has now taken over the investigation."

"That is horrible. An innocent little girl and an old lady were also in there. Oh, my goodness, what about the baby? She has no one."

"That's not true. She has you. I can do whatever is necessary to see to it that child is awarded to you if that's what you want," Cindy proclaims.

"I need air. I have to get out of here."

Making tracks back out the door, I run to my car, collapsing to my knees. Praying aloud, I say, "Lord, this is more than I can bear. I can't handle all of this. My husband played Judas on me with the woman whose death I now mourn. Why, God? Why?"

"You can and you will bear it," my father consoles me as he approaches me.

"Dad, I can't. I have so much hate in my heart there's no way God can bless me."

"It's already in the works. You were unable to conceive, and He is giving you the opportunity to be a mother to this child. Don't you see Him at work?"

"No, I don't. It sounds like you're saying God killed her parents just so I could be her mother. If that's the case, I want no part of it."

"That's not what I'm saying at all. It is horrific what happened to those people. I feel awful about it, but I can't change what happened. The only thing I can do is pray. I'm trying to show you the positive side of things because, no matter what, that child needs a loving parent, and who better to love her like her own than you?"

"How can I be a mother when my marriage is a mess? I can't and don't trust my husband anymore."

"That is a conversation you need to have with him."

"I'm not ready to talk to him."

"Tell him that. You have to communicate. I'm not proud of how things turned out between your mother and me, but one thing for sure is we communicated the good, the bad, and the ugly."

"Thank you, Dad. I love you, and I'm going to make things right between us."

"It has always been in the Lord's hands. He knew when and how to make this moment possible."

Chapter Eighty-two

Ramona Makes A Decision

I hate to do this, but I have to do it for me.

"Delvin, I'm sorry, but I need time. I apologize for upsetting you earlier when you called, but I don't think it's a good idea for you to come here."

"You can't be alone. You need me."

"I did need you, but you ruined that. You hurt me past my soul, and I can't just forgive and forget. I will learn to forgive you one day, but today isn't that day."

"I will go back to the treatment center. I can stay up to six months. That should give you enough time."

"I'm not sure how long I'll need. You've betrayed me in the worst way possible, and you did that mess in our home. I don't care what she said or did. Your love and respect for me should have overruled everything."

"I am so sorry, Mona. I will make things right, and I won't stop until I have you back. I promise I will fix this."

"I just want you to know I'm going to have Cindy help me get custody of Latavia's baby."

"This is what we need."

"No, this is what I want and need. I'm not sure what it is you need, but what I do know is a baby can't and won't fix what you've done. I love you, but I have got to start loving Ramona more. Maybe one day God will make a way for us to make things work. I'm not sure what the future holds for us, but as of right now, I have to make sure my key player is happy and not living in guilt for something I had no control over. You did what you did because that was what you wanted to do. I'm no longer angry with you. I am still hurt, but in time I will heal. Trust is one of the main foundations of a relationship, and you severed that. How do we come back from that? Only God knows. I'm going to put this in His hands because we've already made a mess of things. Take care, my love."

Epilogue

It has been a few months now, and Cindy made it possible for me to get full custody of Lanaya Ramona Michaels. I tried to combine Nariah's and Latavia's names because they're the reason I have this precious angel. As for Delvin and me, we talk daily, write, and send pictures as if we're courting from a distance.

What I have learned to realize is that in life we can't predict or plan our future, because even when we do, it never turns out the way we envisioned it. I have learned so much from my pain, and I no longer allow it to hinder me from moving forward. Delvin and I have a long way to go, and again, I'm uncertain what that means for us, but I refuse to allow it to turn me into a bitter, angry woman. I'm at a happy place in my life right now. I have a successful business and the most beautiful little girl a mother could ask for.

My parents have been great during this process as well. I moved my mom into my house, and she and Dad are working on themselves as well. They have been going to marriage counseling. Dad joins us for dinner every day. He is working on being the husband he knows he can be to Mom. That alone gives me hope. Our last conversation was so uplifting that I too have been going back to church and attending counseling for myself. I am working on my natural and spiritual woman. I can't and won't be able to be who and what I need to be to Lanaya if I continue walking around in bondage.

Only God knows what the future holds for us, but what I do know is that I am on the right track, and the best is yet to come.

The End